Anna Caroline Steele

A Red Republican

An Original Drama

Anna Caroline Steele

A Red Republican
An Original Drama

ISBN/EAN: 9783337376802

Printed in Europe, USA, Canada, Australia, Japan

Cover: Foto ©Andreas Hilbeck / pixelio.de

More available books at **www.hansebooks.com**

A RED REPUBLICAN:

An Original Drama,

IN THREE ACTS.

Dedicated to LADY BARRETT LENNARD, (For whom it was expressly written,)

BY

ANNA C. STEELE.

DECEMBER, 1874

———Si vis me flere, dolendum est Primum ipsi tibi.———

A RED REPUBLICAN.

SCENE.—Versailles and Paris,—Time, 1785-9-90.

~~~~~~~~~~~~~~~

DRAMATIS PERSONÆ.

THE DAUPHIN OF FRANCE......

THE DUC DE ST. PREUX ....

THE VICOMTE ST. LEON ....

THE MARQUIS DE LA ROCHE-JAQUELEIN ....

DR. THORNHILL.. ....

JOSEPH MERRYWEATHER *(English Servant to the Duc de St. Preux*

PAGE TO THE DAUPHIN ....

PIERE LA ROUGE ....

MARCELLE *(A Woman of Brittany*

LIZETTE *(Foster-sister and Domestic to the Duc de St. Preux* ....

LADIES OF THE COURT............

MOB, SOLDIERS, &c., &c. ....

A RED REPUBLICAN.

—◆—

ACT I.

SCENE I.—*The Garden of the Duc de St. Preux's Chateau, near Versailles. House L. Entrance from approach to the House R. (At back) Rustic Seats, after the pattern of the old gardens at Sceaux—a gilt Girandole with flowers, fruit, &c. R. a table set with breakfast, &c., a bundle of un-opened Despatches on table—the seats round the table are house seats, Louis Quatorze—formal but richly furnished.*

LIZETTE, C. ROSETTE, R. LOUISE, L.

are sitting C. *on a rustic seat, making white and pink rose garlands.*

LIZ.—Now girls don't forget what I tell you ; tomorrow is the Duke's wedding day, and as he mayn't get the chance of marrying again, we must make the most of it ; you Rosette must strew white roses in the bride's path—you Louise must hold one end of the garland under which they are to pass, I will hold the other. Being the Duke's foster-sister he naturally gives me the direction of affairs.

Ros.—Is the bride beautiful Miss Lizette ?

LIZ.—I do not know, but the dress is superb ; and that is the chief thing—they say it cost 20,000 francs !

ALL.—How delightful—how happy she must be !

LIZ.—Have the villagers got their offerings ready, Louise ?

LOUISE.—Well, mam'selle, it takes a long time to save something out of nothing so to speak, but by dint of scold-ing and coaxing, the Duke's steward got one family to eco-nomise its bread, another its salt, another its fuel, and so on ; and at last squeezed out the worth of a silver salver on which the bride is to put her gloves.

Ros.—And there's such a beautiful inscription on it the Curé has written, about its being a spontaneous mark of esteem and affection.

Louise.—It seems strange a Duke can't marry without taxing his dependants to provide ornaments ; if the worth of all the finery lavished at weddings was spent in building a hospital or poor-house, what a grand building it would be ; then indeed the brides' would have priceless jewels— the jewels that would shine in grateful hearts and link the donor to heaven by prayers and blessings.

Liz.—Girls you've been flirting with our English butler, Mr. Merryweather ; when a woman changes her politics there's always a man at the bottom of it—you should not listen to him—he is quite a democrat.

Enter Joseph.

Not I, Miss Lizette—there was no need of *my* influence —hunger and cold are your true democrats,—and they monopolise all the eloquence hereabouts. What are you so busy over?

Liz.—Preparing rose-garland for our master's wedding day, Mr. Joseph. Roses you know are emblematic of love.

Jos.—You seem to have left out the most striking por- tions of the emblem.

Liz.—What are they?

Jos.—The thorns—(*takes up a bundle of letters from the table*)—What a heap of despatches there are for the Duke this morning—have his creditors heard of his impending marriage ?

Liz.—No, but his sweethearts have ; they are like a country divided by internal dissensions which yet makes common cause against an invader.

Jos.—I suppose the Duke is very much in love, or he'd never sacrifice so many (including himself) to one.

Liz.—Why should he be in love ?

Jos.—Isn't he going to be married ?

Liz.—That's nothing to do with it, has it girls ?

Ros. & Louise.—Oh *dear*, no.

Liz.—Tell Mr. Joseph what you will marry for. (*To Louise.*)

Louise.—The toilette of course.

Liz.—And you? (*To Rosette.*)

Ros.—Oh-h—the cake—I shouldn't mind how often I married if I got a cake each time.

Jos.—And *you*, Miss Lizette—what would induce *you* to change your state?

Liz.—The wish to *add* to it—I should like to set up a white slave! as for falling in love, as you call it, decent French couples never fall in love until after marriage.

Jos.—And not always with the right persons then, eh? that comes of putting off till to-morrow what had better be done to-day.

Liz.—In *France* our girls are too well brought up to love before marriage. *We* are never allowed to see any man alone to whom we are engaged; *we* don't like short contracts, terminable at will, here; if we lease a plot of ground and a pig—it's for life. We're not like your forward English girls.

Jos.—I suppose not, or else you'd be better able to be trusted.

Liz.—But *your* girls must find it so very easy to be trustworthy.

Jos.—Why so, Miss Lizette?

Liz.—Because the temptation to be otherwise (judging by the specimen I have seen) is so *very* small—ha, ha.

Jos.—My heart is large enough for two—and that's fortunate when one has to deal with a French coquette, who hasn't any at all.

Liz.—Havn't I? Ah, Mr. Joseph, you should hear what my French admirers say.

Jos.—They had better not say too much; there have been English little foxes that have spoiled foreign vines before now, Miss Lizette, and I don't suppose the varmint have lost their teeth, although they're not always shewing them like some people.

Liz.—Girls—Rosette, Louise—we are insulted by this perfidious Englishman; he has impugned the manners of our girls, and the courage of our men. How shall we punish him?

Louise.—Send him back to England to die of endless colds in the head.

Ros.—Keep him here and break his heart.

Liz.—In that case I constitute myself chief executioner; Joseph Merryweather you hear your doom !

Jos.—I answer in the words of the immortal Shakespeare, "Come on Macduff," and—*(they twist the rose chains about him, and bandage his eyes,)* oh ladies, ladies, consider my dignity,— consider my wig,—consider that my master and his friends are coming into breakfast.

Liz.—Will you own we are prettier and better than your English girls.

Jos.—I don't like signing articles of faith with my eyes shut.

Liz.—Well look at me then.

Jos.—I'd rather not, I'm afraid I might do what other great heroes have done for their faith.

Liz.—What is that?

Jos.—Lose my head.

Liz.—Will you own you're no match for a Frenchman.

Jos.— No, but I'll own I'm no match for any woman, let alone three.

Jos.—Now won't you forgive and forget?

Liz.—As a christian I must, as a woman I won't ; good bye Mr. Joseph, I see the company coming.

(He gropes about, the women dodge him.)

Louise, r.—Good bye, Cupid.

Ros. l.—Good bye, Stupid.

Liz.—Which of the heroes of Poetry do you resemble now, Mr. Joseph?

Jos.—I *feel* like " Love among the Roses."

Liz.—You *look* like Bottom among the fairies. Ha, ha.

(Exit.)

Jos.—You good for nothing minxes ! just let me catch you— ah, *do* come and take 'em off, there's a darling Lizette? *(sounds of laughter,)* Miss Lisette, ah, they're taking me off instead; *(aside)* there she is trying to walk heavily, but she can't deceive *me ;* I know her dear little tippetty, tappetty shoes. Oh, there you are, forgive me Lisette, you are the most beautiful of your sex, you are the most virtuous,—

Enter St. Leon.

Jos.—You are the Devil ! *(the bandage falls, and Joseph runs off.)*

St. Leon.—Mad, quite mad—all Englishmen are ! Lizette !

Re-enter Lizette, R.

(He advances—she evades him.)

St. Leon.—Oh I was in hopes *you* had gone mad too.

Liz.—You must excuse Joseph, sir, he meant no harm, he took you for me.

St. Leon.—And why can't you take me for him,—but I suppose the Duc de St. Preux wouldn't admire that, eh?

Liz.—Don't misunderstand my position if you please— I am the Duke's servant and foster-sister—I believe I am almost the only woman of the Duke's acquaintance whom he hasn't made a fool of !

St. Leon.—Good gad, what a fool you must have made of him then ; well, well, all his enjoyment will soon be over—how does he seem—pretty well ?

Liz.—Quite well.

St. Leon.—And cheerful.

Liz.—Gay.

St. Leon.—Well, this is the last comfortable break-fast I may eat with my poor lost friend for some time ; so I must not cloud it with ill omens, but when it's all over you'll see he'll break down !

Liz.—Nay sir, the bride is young, beautiful and rich— why should not my master be happy with, and constant to, Mam'selle De Courcy.

St. Leon.—If he's constant he won't be happy. Besides were she as beautiful as Venus, it must be a dreadful reflection to a man of fashion, to know that he has got something he can never change—never get rid of, however much the gloss is worn off; for my own part I never met a woman worth such a sacrifice, I despise the whole sex.

Liz.—Dear me, sir, I'm afraid they've treated you ill.

St. Leon.—On the contrary, they have adored me !

Liz.—Then you are quite right to despise them.

St. Leon.—At all events they don't treat you so ill when you despise them as they do when you love them ;

so I am the right side of that bargain; but go and tell him that the Vicomte de St. Leon is waiting to offer his condolences and to eat his breakfast.

Liz.—I do not think the Duke is up yet, sir; he has had a bad night.

St. Leon.—Ill?

Liz.—No, cards, but I'll go and see. (*Goes out & returns*)

St. Leon.—Well, is he getting up?

Liz.—He is only getting to the swearing stage at present, Sir; his valet told him you were waiting, and the Duke said you might wait and be—— made as warm as circumstances would permit.

St. Leon.—I'll go to him, he'll be grateful to me afterwards for arousing him. *Going* L.

Liz.—Do, sir; but beware of the first effusion of his gratitude, he will direct it all towards your head.

Exit St. Leon.

These fine Gentlemen spend all their time on themselves, which accounts for their having such a small sense of its value; *(takes up the bundle of letters,)* that's from Lucille, what a goose she is, saying the same thing over and over again, when her having said it once was quite enough to make him tired of her—this other is from a Countess, she is in as great a rage as if she were a fish-woman, all because he is going to marry! I'm sure he never minded *their* being married? but there's no logic in a woman's love, and no love in my master's logic—hey day—here's a name I don't know—"Marcelle"—that must be either a very old or very new affair, or I should have seen the name before now—let me think—if she believes in him it's very new; if she reproaches him, it's very old—well, I don't envy her in either case. Who comes here? a woman, and a peasant woman by her dress. What does she mean by coming to the grand entrance—Hi, my good woman; on looking again in spite of her dress she has something of the air of a Lady—dear me, if she's a Lady, I musn't call her "my good woman."

Enter Marcelle.

Liz.—Have you not come to the wrong entrance, Madame?

MAR.—I was directed to the Chateau St. Preux, is not this it ?

LIZ.—You are not a visitor, are you ?

MAR.—Nay, I am only a traveller seeking information which I was told I might gain here.

LIZ.—Don't you know, Madame, there are always two staircases to a rich man's house. He sometimes demeans himself by using the back stairs ; but he never permits his inferiors to take advantage of *his* !

MAR.—I beg pardon, I will go another way.

LIZ.—No, no ; stay, my master is occupied with a friend, and there is no one to interrupt us ; have you come far?

MAR.—From England.

LIZ.—Why that is Mr. Merryweather's country ; perhaps you can tell me whether they were talking much about him? he is *the* Merryweather you know; the People's hope and the Democrats demi-god—*that's* what he tells me he's called.

MAR.—I have not heard his name.

LIZ.—Oh, but perhaps you were not much at Court or in the Parliament House.

MAR.—No, my life was spent in retirement and study. I only made intimate acquaintance with one Englishman ; a Doctor Thornhill ; he was so kind when I was ill. There is no hero like your English doctor, he battles with more than the dangers of the soldier to meet with less reward.

Liz.—Ah, Madame, but perchance such a man's heart shines more brightly before Heaven than military deco-rations do before men.

MAR.—He was my good angel ; to him I owe employment, respectability, independence ; there was only one of my ills he could not cure, and that was my unhappiness.

LIZ.—Ah ! a man of course was at the bottom of that.

MAR.—When I landed in Brittany I lost sight of Dr. Thornhill ; he came to the French Court to try and cure a dying man. I lingered in my native village haunting the burial place of a dead hope. One night I remembered something the Doctor had said about his practice among the Nobles of the Court ; I resolved to follow him to Versailles ; at daybreak next morning I started :—

Liz.—And whom are you seeking among the French Nobles, a friend?

Mar.—No, Mam'selle, a lover.

Liz.—Ah, you have found out that they don't mean one and the same thing? but do sit down and tell me something about it. If you had said you had a husband who broke your *head* I should have thought nothing of it, *that* is so very common, but a broken heart is always interesting. One never knows when it may happen to oneself, (*sighs*) first, tell me how do *you* define love; what *is* love?

Mar.—Something one feels a great deal too much for some one / much too little worth it generally.

Liz.—And what then is a lover?

Mar.—An insatiable creditor who extorts usury for the most trifling loan, and sells you up at last—but I fear I'm intruding here, and—(*rises.*)

Liz.—(*Pulling her back*) No, no, don't go; the fact is I'm in love myself, and when *that's* the case one *must* prose to somebody! and there's no confidant like a woman; no one but a woman can fathom the unutterable baseness of man; and *that* makes her *so* impartial; when did you first meet him?

Mar.—Five years ago.

Liz.—And you have remembered him all that time, that's 4 years and 11 months too many. What were you doing when you first saw him?

Mar.—I was singing a song.

Liz.—Do you remember what song it was!—but how stupid—of course you do. If you remember the man, of course you won't forget the song.

Mar.—It is a proof that I do; that I have never sung since.

Liz.—(*affected*) Poor thing! and he said he loved you of course; and you believed him, of course, and you thought he was preaching a new Gospel, and he was only plagiarising such a very old fable.

Mar.—Believe him—no, not at first, I did not dare. I was poor, and happiness is so slow in coming to the poor that they may well be half fearful of its rare beauty; but he said it again and again; and what could I do but learn the story by heart; then I whispered it to myself, and by degrees it grew into my memory so indissolubly that Death alone can banish it thence. (*Rises*) At last one day I ran out by myself to the woods that I might cry out, in echo of my joy, "*he loves me, he loves me.*" Such a Sun shone that day as has never shone since !; the birds sang with different notes to those they know now. I forgot that Pain, Suffering or Death were, or ever could be. I only knew there were roses in my breast *he* had gathered, and a memory in my heart *he* had made immortal.

LIZ.—Well, it never had such an effect on me; but perhaps had I been brought up in the country I should have found it dull enough for anything; but oh, Madame, excuse me for saying it, but no man's love *could* have been worth making such a fuss about.

MAR.—If he be not worthy, the greater love does he need.

LIZ.—But he does not always give value in proportion to his needs. Look at those letters; they are all addressed to my master; they are unopened you see; when a man don't open his letters, it is a sure sign that he *is'nt* in love, and *is* in debt.

MAR.—Is your master so much beloved ?

LIZ.—He is adored.

MAR.—What is his charm ?

LIZ.—Indifference I think ; the sex are so perverse !

MAR.—You speak of the sex as it is, vitiated by an artificial existence ; a fine lady does not dislike the excitement of opposition ; her lover's treachery stimulates her vanity, but it cannot quicken that dead nonentity—her heart. In Brittany our love is of another sort ; its glory in success is only to be equalled by its intensity in hate.

LIZ.—Dear me, you don't mean to say you'd resent a man's growing a little tired of one subject, as we're all apt to do.

MAR.—If he were false undesignedly I could forgive him ; if he purposely forsook me, I would bide my hour, and kill him. Oh, I cannot play at love as children do with baubles. I am in earnest or you would not see me here now; give me what help you can, for, if I fail here, I must go on while love and life hold together.

Liz.—What can I do for you?

Mar.—There is a young Breton gentleman visiting here called La Roche-Jaquelein; he used to know the man I seek, he may tell me news of him; let me see him.

Liz.—What was your sweetheart's name?

Mar.—Alas, he gave me a false one; at least I suppose so, for I never could hear anything of him at the Chateau where he used to come on shooting expeditions, and my letters have never been answered.

Liz.—Ah, *those* poor things, letters (pointing to packet) they will never be *read*, much less *answered*. Why don't you apply to my master the Duc de St. Preux? he knows all the villains—I beg their pardon; all the Nobles of the Country; he is not ill natured where himself is not concerned, and would give up a friend with the greatest magnanimity in the world.

Mar.—When and how can I see him?

Liz.—This evening he will be alone for a short time while his friends are dressing for a Court ball, which they all mean to attend. Be here at eight o'clock, and I will station you where you cannot fail to get speech of him; but do not detain him too long, for these great people don't like to be delayed in their pursuit of pleasure.

Mar.—How can I thank you?

Liz.—Wait until you know whether you are not more inclined to upbraid me; the proverb, "ignorance is bliss," was invented for lovers. Even, if you attain your object, are you certain to prize it as highly as you fancy you will? should you know your old love again if he stood before you now? Could you heart warm to him as of old?

Mar.—I will answer you in the words of a beautiful old heathen fable; a wandering Prince loved and deserted a Thracian Princess; she watched the sea line until hope was dead—then the Gods, in pity, changed her into an almond tree. One winter the lover came back and vainly called her name; they showed him the tree then bare of foliage and blighted by frost, but when he flung his arms about it, the poor sere plant burst into leaf and blossom at the late touch of his heart   *Exit.*

Liz.—I begin to think that I can't have valued Joseph

↑ they'll go into the waste-paper basket
   ′′....′ with the unpaid bills.

half enough ; but then he hasn't deserted me yet !!!
Here comes the Duke, I'll give this Marcelle's letter a
chance by putting it on the top. Poor thing, perhaps she
takes it to heart as badly as that unhappy woman who
has just gone.   *(Exit.)*

Enter St. Preux *and* St. Leon, L.

St. P.—My dear St. Leon don't apologise—one's sweetheart can't come too early; one's creditor can't come too
late, one's friend can't come amiss at any hour. Talking
of friends you will meet an old Breton acquaintance presently, Henri De La Roche-Jaquelein ; he is coming up
from the country on purpose to attend my nuptials to-
morrow.

St. L.—Ah, some men have such a morbid fancy for
witnessing executions !

St. P.—But at least you will be glad to see an old
friend after so long an absence.

St. L.—No doubt I shall be delighted, but I shan't
know what on earth to say to him.

St. P.—Abuse some other mutual friend such as myself, that will soon make you feel eloquent.

St. L.—But La Roche-Jaquelein is one of those en-
thusiastic fools who can see no fault in an old friend
such as yourself.

St. P.—Then do *you* guard his friendship, St. Leon, as
a pearl beyond price ; no one can be in greater want
of such a friend ; oh, here he comes, now I shall get an
honest greeting.

St. L.—Now I shall get my breakfast.

Enter De La Roche-Jaquelein, *from back*, (L.)

St. P.—St. Leon, this is a double pleasure ; it warms
my heart to the core to see you both again.

St. L.—How dy'e do ; the breakfast is getting cold.

St. P.—I'm very grateful for such a proof of your
interest in me—you have had a very long ride.

De La Roche.—No ride is long when a friend is at
the end of it ; I'm quite of old Horace's opinion :

Nil ego contulerim jucundo sanus amico.

But you, St. Preux, can never have been less inclined to
admit the supremacy of friendship now that you are ab-

sorbed by the pressing claims of love.

St. L.—*Those* are not his most pressing claims. He has exchanged Venus' brazen yoke for Hymen's, because the latter is made of Gold.

De La Roche.—Don't ask me to believe that my friend would sell himself.

St. L.—No—I don't quite say *that*—but I'm sure he would make an accommodation of himself, to circumstances.   *(they sit.)*

De La Roche.—I hope that we shall henceforth have you for a neighbour in Brittany. I suppose you will settle in the country?

St. P.—My dear fellow, when a lazy carrier excused himself to that sapient Greek—Xenophon—for digging a grave for a wounded soldier he was tired of carrying, with the plea, "We must all die!" Xenophon answered, "Yes, we must all die, but we needn't be buried alive!"—no, I shall not live in the country!

St. L.—You see St. Preux's melancholy state! he is as dull as a fish, or an Englishman.

St. P.—Don't abuse the English, St. Leon; there has been at least one man, one Monarch of their race, for whom I entertain the profoundest respect.

De La Roche.—You mean King Henry V. of heroic memory? he who wrote Agincourt in English History, with English arrows for a pen, and alas! the best blood in France for Ink.

St. P.—I allude to King Henry VIII., of conjugal memory, he understood Women, and his Countrymen's estimation of them *so* well, always went straight to the point.

St. L.—You mean he always sent *them* to the point—no man better understood the art of cutting an inconvenient acquaintance dead.

St. P.—Yes, but see how popular he was and his method too!!—to the present day it survives (with variations) among the lower classes of the English, and while to knock over a hare is felony, wives and vermin are unprotected by the law.

St. L.—You would not compare a man's sport with his penance?—The law-givers' want to knock over the hares' themselves, while they are often ridden over rough shod by their wives—its the common law, not of England only, but of nature, that of reprisals.

DE LA ROCHE.—Do not forget there is an Englishman present, that man yonder who officiates as St. Preux's butler.

ST. P.—What. Joseph Merryweather there, whom I trust so implicitly with my cellar because he doesn't like French wines ? he is only a servant, and has no business to remember of what country he is ; *a slave first and an Englishman afterwards*, that should be his motto.

DE LA ROCHE.—But we must not forget that we are gentlemen, and good breeding is like the beauty of Helen,—of all countries.

ST. P.—He shall speak for himself, Hi, Joseph, were men murdering their wives as much as usual when you were last at home ?

Jos.—I didn't notice any change my Lord Duke—excepting that it was the women seemed fonder than ever !

ST. P.—Of their husbands ?

Jos.—Of aggravating them, my Lord—the more a women loves you the worse she aggravates you !

ST. P.—And does she love the manual punishment you inflict for her sins ?

Jos.—My Lord, she glories in it ; just try and interfere when a couple are enjoying 'emselves in a snug little row ; try and come between a woman and her two pet black eyes, and see which of the three will get the worst of *that* quarrel.

ST. P.—That will do Joseph, you have borne testimony to your national peculiarities.

Jos.—Yes, my Lord Duke, and I shall be as proud to do as much for your country any day ; which kicking and scratching is its worst point in rows.

DE LA ROCHE.—When I came to Paris I expected to find the St. Preux I used to know ; the man who rode, wrestled, fenced and made love with the best of us. Do you ride now, St. Preux ? I am quite disheartened to find you so altered, you used to be a man and now you have faded into a fine gentleman.

ST. P.—There are some very fine well-trained hackneys

in my stables, I believe.

De La Roche.—Horses turned into automata you mean, machines that some one else has screwed up for you and sets going at a given word. I would make a present of such to the first old invalid lady I knew to be in want of gentle exercise ; give me the horse who *lives* under you, who shows courage which I can praise, strength and speed I can test, temper which I can parly with (my dear St. Preux, I would not give a straw for either a horse or a woman who didn't show a little temper) and vice, which I can fight and conquer; not that a man should be in *too* great a hurry to find out his wife's or his horse's ill-humour, ten to one he gets implicated as having begun the quarrel himself.

St. L.—Excuse the interruption, are you married ?

De La Roche.—I have not that pleasure yet.

St. L.—That's why you call it a pleasure, you'll know better bye and bye.

De La Roche.—Do you speak from experience ?

St. L.—No, but I've studied that of other men, from the vantage ground of impartial celibacy, and I tell you my idea of a wife, she can be expressed musically as a *bar*, architecturally as a *ruin*, entomologically as a *gad fly*, agriculturally as a blight, grammatically as a *full stop* to all one's pleasures.

De La Roche.—I'll tell you what *I* imagine her to to be ; a musical concord to close a man's life in harmony with heaven's spheres; a pure temple in which he may enshrine his worthiest thoughts ; a butterfly only, inasmuch as she is the emblem of that better part of him, his soul ! a harvest that will live garnered in his heart when earthly grain perish in frost and storm ; and to parallel your simile to the end grammatically, the hyphen that unites two names, two natures, two lives in one unbroken link of mutual love and esteem !

St. L.—How refreshing youth and enthusiasm would be, if they were not so absurd !—you provincials would believe in anything—Priests' Petticoats and Prime Ministers !

De La Roche.—But even my credulity has its limits, for I put no faith in Pagans, Popinjays or Parisians.

St. L.—Perhaps you would place greater faith in the metal of this sword—(*half draws*).

De La Roche.—It is the only thing about you worth putting faith in ; I should be delighted to test its reality. (*draws.*)

St. P.—Hey day, is this the way you cement an old friendship; put up your swords—are you not aware that there's nothing in the world worth fighting about ?

De La Roche.—*I* am a modest man, and can't put myself first in anything but what concerns my honour !

St. L.—The great can afford to be magnanimous, besides it would be absurd to pit a valuable life like mine against that of a fossil, a half alive Provincial ; here's my hand.

De La Roche.—I should have been more honored by your sword, but—here is mine. (*they shake hands.*)

St. P.—As it seems impossible to discuss woman even in the abstract, without quarrelling, let us talk about something only one of us is interested in, then we shall agree—tell me about your favourite horse De La Roche-Jaquelein, what is its especial charm.

De La Roche.—Wickedness—It was only the other day that after he had tried everything he knew, and invented a good deal he did not know that, growing tired of discussion, he ran away with me with as much spirit as though he had been an Irishman and I a beautiful woman.

St. P.—Reversing my system exactly ; I run away with them first and grew tired of them afterwards—where did your ride stop ?

De La Roche.—On the edge of a cliff, when it came to smelling the salt water and hearing the hiss of the waves in the whirlwind of speed in which I seemed moving, I thought it time to make it up with my nag, which I did by hitting him hard, naturally he was surprised and indignant, and stopped to kick—oh, he is the most delightful horse in the world.

St. L.—The moral is, if you want to succeed with women or horses, take them by surprise first and hit them hard afterwards, but it wouldn't succeed with me ; for I am never surprised at anything, never, not even at my own success.

DE LA ROCHE.—My dear St. Leon, I did not dream of comparing you to a horse or to any other domestic and useful animal, but tell me more of my old friend here—does he wrestle now?

ST. L.—Yes, in the spirit, with his creditors.

DE LA ROCHE.—Does he love?

ST. L.—Himself devoutly.

DE LA ROCHE.—Does a man of society *only* take an interest in himself?

ST. L.—There isn't any time in society for taking an interest in anyone else.

DE LA ROCHE.—There, you give the explanation of revolutions and the apology of rebels?

ST. P.—Rebels, there are no such things, why should there be; are not we all pretty comfortable barring ennui, certainly; I have been at death's door from the effects of boredom!

ST. L.—He must get the English doctor to prescribe for you; he comes from a country where men bore their friends, but never themselves; they are so vulgarly active.

ST. P.—Oh, by the way, yes—I asked Doctor Thornhill to visit me here to-day, he saved my life once, so I feel myself obliged to ask him to dinner now and then.

ST. L.—That rough brusque islander coming? I would have put on an extra cloak had I known; I always feel when in an Englishman's presence, as if in that of an east wind. (*shivers affectedly.*)

Enter Thornhill.

DR. T.—The east wind did you say, certainly it is fatal to exotics. Talking of exotics, how is my patient to day?

ST. P.—Oh, doctor I'm wretchedly ill.

DR. T.—Umph, let's see, you are young.

ST. P.—For a Frenchman, yes.

DR. T.—True, a Frenchman is never young.

ST. P.—And never old.

DR. T.—What is your worst symptom?

ST. P.—Fatigue.

DR. T.—How did it first show itself?

ST. P.—Well, after I'd tried every liquor under the sun and got equally drunk on them all; after I'd told the same lie to some fifty different women; after I'd fought a dozen duels with wearisome success, at last everything began to pall on me, isn't it sad!

DR. T.—It is, indeed, pitiable!

ST. P.—The fact is, I did everything *too* well; drank too well, loved too well, fought too well—for my part I can't think how La Roché-Jaquelein there, who lives in the country where they do nothing well, except stagnate, can support existence.

DE LA ROCHE.—Perhaps you've never tried my receipt against stagnation.

ST. P.—*Have* you one? pray let me have a copy of it.

DE LA ROCHE.—Serve the King; guard my honour; love a woman. I find that to practice these three virtues keeps me very actively employed.

ST. P.—Oh, thank you—well, yes, perhaps you'll be kind enough to give it to my valet, *he* practises all *my* virtues for me.

ST. L.—He must have quite a sinecure.

ST. P.—Then you may be sure he don't deserve it. It is part of the condition of sinecures that the holders' should not do so. La Roché-Jaquelein will you attend the court fête with us?

DE LA ROCHE.—Not I! I have a parade to attend, one or two Vendeans like myself are forming a corps, that we may be able, if called upon to serve the King, in a more substantial form, than by bowing to him at his court balls. I have already secured some of the best youngsters of the court, who would die for his Majesty,—but who won't go to the Provinces to be trained; so we meet near Versailles every half year, and are inspected by an old follower of Turenne's. After all its something to be prepared, even for a chance of being useful—will you join us St. Leon?

ST. L.—Me—be useful—thank you, no. I know too well what is due to my station.

DE LA ROCHE.—At least come and see us parade, it will soon be over, the drum will beat to quarters, and we shall all chorusing the retreat.

(Song, La Retraite.)

But, understand, the retreat is a song we only sing before our friends; for our enemies we shall have a different tune—the tune which is followed by the silence of death, that of the advance. *(exeunt omnes.)*

Lizette and Joseph enter and clear away some of the breakfast appanage.

Liz.—What is the matter, Monsieur Merryweather?

ital Jos.—I don't know, unless (sighs) I have got an affection of the heart!

Liz.—Dear me, is that a melancholy complaint?

Jos.—Shocking, unless you're sure of your girl,—which you never are until you have ceased to care to be so.

Liz.—Have you often suffered from it?

Jos.—Often, and each time worse than the last.

Liz.—How does it show yourself, in *you?*

Jos.—Makes me look like a fool to one person, and act like a brute to everyone else; but I don't care to talk about it Miss Lizette, they say talking of the toothache is sure to bring it on.

Liz.—But, perhaps, I might find a cure.

Jos.—Thank ye, Miss, but I'm afraid I couldn't afford the fee.

Liz.—What is that?

Jos.—Matrimony.

Liz.—Don't you ever mean to marry, Mr Joe?

Jos.—Not until I can help it Miss; but I'm afraid the women will be one too many for me some day; a wife might interfere with my missions.

Liz.—Your what?

Jos.—My mission—I've two of them you know; one is to fall in love with every pretty girl I meet, that's what I call an involuntary mission and comes of itself; the other is a patriotic purpose; the redemption of my enslaved countrymen; to *that*, when I was at home, I devoted all my eloquence, all my time, and a good deal of my savings. The eloquence went to prove that all men are equal, and that I ought to have a servant to wait on me, instead of acting as such. The savings went in beer and baccy to the other patriots, who used to cheer my speeches. Oh, Miss, I wish you could have heard the uproarious 'Ear,' 'Ear's,' they shook the roof of the Black Lion, when I said "Down with taxes; down with William Pitt; down with the King!"

Liz. And *did* they down with him?

Jos. Why no, they did'nt. He came in procession through the town the next day, and the very rascals who had promised to give all their energies and lives to undermining the throne, accepted a contract to build some remarkably strong oak chairs for one of the Royal Palaces; they didn't even put in the nails wrong side upwards.

Liz. What excuse did they make?

Jos. They said they didn't believe the King was a bad sort of chap after all; but the real fact was I had no more cash left for beer and pipes, so I had to condescend to hunt out an old master of mine, one of the pampered aristocrats of my country who debase their menials by enervating kindness, and ask him for a character. I told him I had reasons to wish to live abroad; he little guessed he was ex-patriating a second Oliver Cromwell. He asked me in that insulting civil way of his, if it was Love or Law I was running away from, and then gave me a recommendation to the Duke here, and here I am—but ere long, perhaps, Joseph Merryweather may doff the menial plush for the Imperial purple.

Liz. Oh, Mr. Jo. I'm sure the liveries are very, *very* becoming.

Jos. They are! but I must sacrifice personal advantages to public interest, and the sacrifice may be more imminent than you imagine, Miss Lizette. I could tell you a secret, if you weren't a woman, I *would* tell you a secret; but then it wouldn't be one any longer.

Liz. But if I weren't a woman you wouldn't want to tell it to me. Mr. Joseph, you might tell me a little, a very little corner of it.

Jos. Hist—well—there's going to be a rising.

Liz. Of the moon you mean; she will soon be at the full.

Jos. This is no case of moonshine, and there's more than one man in it. I daren't say any more just now, but if ever any trouble comes to this country, don't forget you can have a friend and a home in mine.

. Liz. If any misfortune should ever come to this country, Mr. Joe, I should *not* take that moment to forget that it is my home.

Jos. Lizette, before we part, let me feel that we are one in this great undertaking. Swear to unite with us to break the bonds of the oppressed and the heads of the oppressors.

Liz. Well, Mr. Joe, I've been brought up on the estate. My mother was nurse to the Duke; he has always been kind to me, and I shouldn't like to have his head broken until I saw what sort of one the next comer might have. You see, I have been in service here all my life.

Jos. In service—there's a term to be applied to a human being, who has equal rights with any *other* human being. The Duke ought not to have made *a* servant of you at all.

Liz. Law! Mr. Joe, do you think he ought to have made a Duchess of me!!!!

Jos. (severely) *A sister!* he ought to have made *a sister* of you, Miss Lizette!

Liz. He couldn't do that, Joe, you know, for he was an only child, and no one could ever say anything against that sainted old man, his father, the late Duke.

Jos. The very word servant means servus, a serf or slave. When I started patriotism, Miss Lizette, I learned a little latin—a little goes a long way with patriots, you see, they don't quite know what it means, and they don't know what they mean themselves, and so it's all what you French call on a cord.

Liz. Well, Mr. Joe, to please you, I have no objection to vowing destruction to tyrants and dukes in general, with the exception of those I've known myself in particular.

Jos. Let us swear (with hand in hand, which will be pleasant as well as effective). Let us swear never to hold any terms with the domineerial race, but to take every opportunity of thwarting and destroying its authority! (*Together*) Agreed. Down with dukes and despots ; down with——

Enter St. Preux C.; *comes down calling " Joe, Lizette."*

Liz. Jos. (*together*). Yes, sir—certainly, sir—what did you please to want—yes my, my Lord—I'm sure, I beg ten thousand pardon, your Grace.

St. P. I am sure you require no pardon. I hope I do not grudge any domestics their harmless confidences with each other ; you have not found me a harsh master, have you, my foster-sister ?——

Liz. In justice to myself, I must say I made an exception in your favour.

Jos Oh yes, she owned your Grace was the best of the bunch.

St. P. (*surprised*). Why, has there been any cause of complaint against me ?

Liz. Not on my side, I assure you, sir.

Jos. And I have no personal objection to my Lord Duke.

St. P. I am glad you are all happy and satisfied—for my part, I never believe in all the absurd exaggerations that abound concerning the discontent of the lower classes. The people on my estate always take off their hats to me.—What more do I want?

Jos. No, I dare say your Grace requires nothing more. (*aside*) Lizette, you'll see that those who took off their hats the lowest will be the most eager to take off their patron's heads.

St. P. Joseph, my shoe buckle is unfastened—kneel down and put it right (*seats himself hesitating*).

Jos. *What* a position for Joseph Merryweather, the people's Joseph. Oh that all aristocracy had but one foot, and I could tread on its corns !

St. P. Now, then, make haste. I'm afraid your knees are growing stiff, Joseph. (*Pokes him with his sword*).

Jos. (*going down rapidly*). Directly, my Lord Duke, it shall be done directly. Will your Grace kindly put away that nasty thing. I've an hereditary objection to swords. My mother didn't like 'em before I was born.

St. P. Lizette, fasten this bow on my coat lappet. You have no hereditary objection to bows, have you ?

Liz. No, sir, I've a natural affinity to them.

Jos. (*aside to her as she kneels*). Lizette, Is THIS "*thwarting his authority ?*"

Liz. (*aside*). Joseph, is *this* "*defying his mandates ?*"

St. P. Now, you may go to your respective duties, and be careful they are fulfilled properly. A good servant should have no interest next his master's. Joseph, see that my court wig is properly dressed.

Jos. (*aside*). Oh ! that it were the head, St. P., eh ?

Jos. Directly, sir, directly (*running off*).

St. P. (to Lizette). And see that my lace ruffles are in order for me to wear.

Liz. (*aside*). Oh ! that I could wear 'em myself, St. P., eh ?

Liz. You shall have them at once, my Lord Duke.

Lizette and Joseph meet at back of Stage.

Jos. Lizette.

Liz. Joseph.

Jos. Let's swear it again when we get outside.

Liz. If you don't think he will hear.   (*Exeunt.*)

St. P. What willing devils those servants of mine are ! nearly 8 o'clock ! it is time for me to go and dress—heigho—when any crisis affects the life of an Englishman, he eats a dinner to accommodate it ; a Frenchman under similar circumstances makes an oration or an epigram for variety. I'll try my hand at an epitaph, " Here lies Francois de St. Preux, whose lies were only equalled by the credulity of womankind." Oh, well, I've done with women now, for a wife is an institution better than a woman ; in my case, she's an asylum for the indigent. I dare say I shall like her, for she's pretty enough ; had she only been any other man's wife I could have adored her ! I was *very nearly* in love once with a sweetheart of my own *(Marcelle enters at back)* and there's no telling what follies I might not have committed ; fortunately we were parted, and as we shall never meet again I can afford to feel a little sentimental about her, especially as I'm going to marry another woman !

(Marcelle speaks from back of stage, " Francois" in a hushed, suppressed voice).

St. P.   Who speaks my christian name so glibly ?

Mar.   A woman who has called no other man by his since she last saw you ; Francois, it is I, it is Marcelle.

St. P.   *(stupified)* Marcelle !

Mar.   Yet though your unspoken name has been in my thoughts so long, I hardly dare echo it now ; you have cheated me so often, you have answered me in my dreams ; you have called me in lonely roads ; you have haunted me with illusions, and now I feel as ﬅ though reality itself were mania.   Speak to me Francois, call my name with love in your tone that I may feel that life and light are coming back to my numbed heart.

St. P.   Marcelle, do not ask me to speak to you, when silence is the best mercy I can show you.

Mar.   Mercy ! yes, I *can* believe in mercy now.   A Pæan is rising in my heart—I feel as if my thanksgiving would thrill the angels—Heaven is kind—Heaven be praised, for *I* am saved, now *you* are found.

St. P.   *(aside)* What can I say to her—why *will* women feel so much.   Marcelle, it is so long since I saw you that you must not be surprised.

Mar.   Long! ah, love, if the time seemed long to you, time for me was annihilated. I feel as if I had been dead all these years' and was suddenly reanimated by a soul — something full of infinite pain and extacy—but why did you kill me for so long a time, Francois ? and oh, the agony of the first days of death and loss ; I was strong and bright then ; I could weep ; could clench my hands, could sob out your name in my sleep—then my eyes grew dim with watching the road ; my hands dropped and even my footsteps ceased to wear a path in the weary woodland where last we met.

St. P.   Would that we had never met.

Mar.   You can say *that*—ah, you have forgotten how happy we were—you think I am reproaching you for the past—oh, my love, all reproach dies in the divine moment of re-union— they mocked me, Francois—you remember Jeanette, whom I hated because you called her pretty—how she smiled as time went on and you came no more. "Aha, you have lost your fine sweetheart," she cried—"look ! it is spring ! bird calls to bird—look, flowers leaves—but *Marcelle is alone.*" I struck her in the face because her words were true, and then I hid my own and despaired.

ST. P. Marcelle, I cannot atone, forgive me ; and—

MAR. Hush, all is atoned—oh, mine own, I have got you again—my soul is come back to its body, and I'm the happiest woman alive; oh, so happy, so happy (*throws herself on his neck.*)

ST. P. (*gravely*) You did not hear all I wished to say, my poor Marcelle ; I said forgive me—I must add, forget me !

MAR. Are you turned to stone that your words are so cold; you were kinder in my dreams, for then you always smiled a welcome to my outstretched arms.

ST. P. Consider—when a man adjures a woman to forget their past, does it not mean that, for them, there can be no future ?

MAR. And what but death can part us now—I have prayed to die—but to-day I feel as if an age would be too short to taste my joy in.

ST. P. Law, which is nearly as strong as death, can part us.

MAR. What question of law can arise between us ?—Love shall be the sole adjudicator between you and me—we will love with the glow of our youth—the force of our prime, and when age has left us with no more chance or grace in ourselves ; love shall still make us beautiful to each other—why do you not speak, *Francois ?*

ST. P. Perhaps because it is difficult to resign all that *might* have been to all that *must* be—farewell. (*going, she clings to him*).

MAR. No—oh, no—you shall not go—what, is that terrible time coming over again—those pale, sickly hours of our severance—what do you mean ?—I do not, (*pause*) I DARE not understand you !

Enter Joseph, R. (*La Roche-Jaquelein, St. Leon, Lizette and Thornhill, from back.*)

Jos. If you please, my Lord Duke, I—beg your pardon, I'm sure, my Lord Duke—didn't know you had. company, (*aside*) (I see it's never too late not to mend) but a message has come from the Duchess as is to be, and she wants to see you immediately.

St. L. (*aside*, Not much too soon I should say.) (*to* Dr. Thornhill) Quite a case of Ariadne and Theseus, eh?

Dr. T. My only regret for not having lived in Theseus's time is, that I missed the pleasure of kicking that gentleman.

St. L. Ariadne wouldn't have thanked you for that; women like to do all the punishing themselves—besides, there was Bacchus, you know. (*advances jauntily to Marcelle*) "Let *me* be your Bacchus, Madame?"
(*Marcelle puts him aside, and says, in a concentrated dull voice,* "Who is it who has sent for you, Francois?"

Jos. His Lordship's Bride, ma'am; she is a little—um —out of sorts.

St. L. Don't alarm yourself, St. Preux, she's only ill—in her temper; because the family jewels you promised to send her haven't arrived—says she can't and won't be married without them.

Mar. Whose is this bride of whom are you all talking? (*walks up to the group*) WHICH OF YOU GENTLEMEN IS ABOUT TO BE MARRIED? (*they look at St. Preux—he looks down, she follows the direction of their eyes*).

Mar. You!

Dr. T. My dear, you had better come away.

Mar. Is it YOU?—say it isn't true, Francois—say it isn't true—say it with your own lips, and let me curse them for liars—what is this they say you are about to do?

St. P. They say what is truth. I am about to marry a lady of rank, equal to—of fortune more than my own— we are to be married to-morrow.

Mar. Oh, oh, do you love her?

St. P. I shall marry her.

Mar. You must not, *shall* not marry her—it must be broken off—gentlemen, tell him that a noble must not be less than his name—that a christian cannot forsake a poor wretch whose only earthly hope is in him?

St. P. You ask me—a gentleman and a Peer of France—to break his plighted word !

Mar. *I* have no reason to think you would find it difficult to do so.

St. P. I have never broken my word—at least not to my equals.

Mar. I see—*gentlemen* have *two* words of honour—one incorruptible for the equal who *can* enforce its observance—the other corrupt and worthless, pledged only to the helpless and unprotected—excuse my ignorance gentlemen, I am of what is called the *lower* class, I have been used to trust to the plain yea and nay of the poor. I have risen in the social scale, I know now what it is to have been loved by a Duke and lied to by a villain !

St. P. (*annoyed*) Madame, there was more force in your grief than in your anger.

Mar. But more truth in my anger ! But see I am *not* angry—I am calm—only very helpless, very sorrowful —pity my helplessness— reward my constancy—tell your bride that you cannot marry her, for you are *mine !*

St. L. Impossible, Madame ; think what people would say.

La Roche. Think of the bride, Madame.

Liz. Think of the trousseau—oh, it's quite impossible.

St. P. I cannot, Marcelle ; you prolong a painful scene in vain—your friend I shall always be, (*takes her hands, she tears them away*) if you will let me—I acknowledge that I gave you my heart—but that was long since. To-day, the gift would not be worth your having, even if I could renew it—now will you say farewell kindly and—go ?

Mar. (*cowers away from his outstretched hand*) Oh, that I had died—had died before I knew this hour—before I saw him again—at least I loved my dreams, at least I nursed my hope ; now all is lost ! lost ! ! lost ! ! !

Dr. T. You will not wait for him to repeat his dismissal, Marcelle ? Save yourself from further insult, and go—as he says.

Mar. Yes, I will go—as *he* says—but *I shall return*—remember that, Francois.

St. P. You will be welcome, Madame, if you are *then* resigned to the force of circumstances.

Mar. Shall I be welcome? we shall see—I call you all and Heaven, which is above all, to witness that I, who found my way to this man through my great love, will never cease to dog him with great hate—my injury is one of many ; the hate of a whole people smoulders under your feet—some touch more reckless than the rest—some firebrand of wrong, hurled by a wanton hand, will make all France a hideous conflagration—then the proud heads will go down with the humble—then will the Palace be levelled lower than the peat-hut—then women who have have loved and lost, as I have loved and lost, will have their revenge—then the souls you have made black shall throw their shadows over yours—the lives *you* have made hard shall grind yours to powder—*I shall return*—be sure of that, and on *that* day I shall remember *this !*

St. Preux.   Marcelle.   Thornhill.
De La Roche.   St Leon.
Joseph.   Lizette.

Curtain.

ACT II.

Scene I.—*The Dauphin's schoolroom at Versailles. The room is hung with maps and furnished with globes, books labelled " Royal Roads to Learning," &c.*

Lizette *discovered arranging books and papers.*

Liz. I came in the hope of meeting Monsieur Merry-weather by accident, and I've waited here at least an hour on purpose (*looks at clock*), that clock says I've only waited ten minutes, that clock is too slow ; besides when one is in love or going to be hanged, an hour or ten minutes seems equally painful. Here he comes. I hope I shan't show him how glad I am to see him again.

My grandmother used to say no properly behaved girl is ever glad to see her lover !—I'm afraid I shall never be properly behaved.

Enter JOSEPH.

Jos. What my Lizette—but I must remember my mission, and not feel too much.

LIZ. What my Jose—but I must remember my grandmother, and not show too much.

Jos. How nice she looks. Blow the mission ; Lizette.

LIZ. Sir.

Jos. She must love me—she's so cursedly disagreeable. I wish I could think of something new and striking to say.

LIZ. I wish I could think of something to say—one looks so foolish when one's dumb—besides it's so out of character with a woman

Jos. Now for an inspiration. Miss Lizette, it's—it's. I feel that it's—it's.

LIZ. Yes, you feel that it's—it's.

Jos. Fine weather for the time of year, isn't it, Miss?

LIZ. Rather too cold, don't you think ? I prefer it a little warmer myself.

Jos. Don't you hear what the ring doves are saying, Miss Lizette? they say—at least he says—do—oo—do—ooo—do,ooo.

LIZ. And don't you know what my cat Minette says, Mr. Joseph? Sha-want—sha-want—sha-want.

Jos. Here comes the Dauphin, just my luck ; somebody always does interrupt me just when I'm beginning to know what to say.

LIZ. Mr. Joseph, when things are worth saying they come of themselves; but tell me, are you as great a democrat as ever?

Jos. Greater than ever since I came to court—didn't—St. Preux get me appointed pugilistic Professor-in-Chief to H. R. H. the Dauphin. Don't they do their best to degrade me by luxury? If I weren't a patriot, I might have so far forgotten myself as to be grateful, but I know what is due to my principles.

Liz. And I know what is due to my Prince—I too have been promoted by the Duke's influence. I am pocket handkerchief holder of the second rank to H.R.H. the Dauphin—and although I am a court domestic, I never keep the royal nose waiting more than ten minutes at the most.

Jos. There is a strange variance in our duties, Lizette; my office is to afflict, yours is to console the royal proboscis! it's allegorical of our differing politics; and who is that who is walking backwards before the Dauphin?

Liz. Don't you remember the Vicomte St. Leon. The Duke got him promoted too.

Jos. What wholesale jobbery. I must say these aristocrats do it handsomely when they once begin to corrupt. I couldn't do it better myself; but we will repay them.

Liz. Then I hope it will be in their own coin, but you must not be seen here until you're sent for.

Jos. But I'm just beginning to feel so very eloquent.

Liz. Go.

Jos. And so, very.——

Liz. Go, I tell you.

Jos. And so very sure you love me?

Liz. I swear I don't. —How did you find it out?

Jos. Any one could have seen it with half an eye. *Exit.*

Enter The Dauphin, *accompanied by a Page, preceded by* St. Leon, *who bows towards him and produces a large Map.*

St. Leo. Will your R.H. please to cast your eyes on this nice easy map?

Dau. I can't, I'm so tired (*reclines languidly on a couch and plays at cup and ball.* Page *and* Lizette *station themselves behind him.*

Liz. Poor fellow, of course he is; there's nothing so fatiguing as doing nothing all day.

St. Leo. Your Royal Highness perceives that this globe represents the world, and is round; do you know what makes it round?

Dau. Yes, love.

St. Leo. Your Royal Highness has mastered the first rudiments of physical science. With regard to this map, your royal parents insist that you should be perfect in geography—at the same time I have directions on no account to over fatigue your Royal Highness by urging you to persevere ; perhaps if your Royal Highness's Page would look at it, it would be sufficient.

Page. That is the map of Europe. That large space (*pointing to the Map*) is France. Those smaller specks represent the use of the civilised world.

Dau. Of course—I know that.

St. Leo. Admirably learnt indeed, what precocity ! what genius ! Pray remember to say exactly the same thing to your royal parents when they see you to-day, and enquire of your progress.

Dau. And I shall be King of France.

St. L. But you needn't remember to repeat *that*, your royal papa might think you were in a hurry.

Dau. But papa is no King, I heard mamma say so. When they brought him back from Paris, the other day, and he wore the national tricolour, she said he was a Plebeian.—Now a Plebeian isn't a king—is he ?

St. L. Well, no—but sometimes a king may be a Plebeian. There's a vulgar monarch over the water who eats his own mutton, and is constant to his own wife. A real king should live on his subjects' mutton, and be constant to *their* wives !

Enter Joseph *dressed in a plain dark court suit. He has a bag with him containing boxing-gloves.*

St. L. And what do you teach ?

Jos. Dumb eloquence in the English language, my Lord. (*produces gloves.*)

Jos. Is your Royal Highness ready to take your English lesson ?

St. L. Hey, day, Joseph, since when have you turned Professor ?

Jos. Since the aristocrats became so ignorant, my Lord Viscount.

Sr. L. What barbarity; but, of course, you do not touch the Dauphin.

Dau. Oh, no; I always win, don't I, Joseph?

Jos. I flatter myself, sire, that I haven't lived at Court for nothing.

Liz. Stop! His Royal Highness is about to sneeze! The Royal precedent must be observed—it follows that we must all sneeze. The page is paid the lowest, consequently he must sneeze the loudest. Now Professor Merryweather, you may proceed.

After a short round, during which the Dauphin leads off, and the Page counters every return blow, the Dauphin flings down the gloves.

All. Bravo! your Royal Highness!

Sr. L. What spirit—what courage; I am glad I'm not his Royal Highness's enemy.

Liz. And I am glad I'm not his Royal Highness's page.

Sr. L. Will your Royal Highness essay Father Rubric's rapid race to Latin, or Herr Smichdt's garrulous guide to German, or Professor Perk's "Perseverance put into a Pea-pod."

The Dau. I won't learn anything more—I'll play chess with Lizette.

Liz. Oh, your Royal Highness, consider my place is to hold the royal handkerchief to your more royal nose, it is impossible I can be guilty of such a neglect of my office.

Dau. I'll play chess with Lizette.

St. L. Your Royal Highness is aware that a breach of etiquette is the one fault strictly forbidden by your royal parents and tutors.

Dau. That's just why I want to do it.

Sr. L. And that your poor page here must be punished severely for your disobedience.

Dau. Oh, he's used to it.

Jos. (*to Lizette*) what do they punish the plebeian for the Prince's sins?

Liz. (*aside*) What else are plebeians for?

Jos. They are finding out their uses, Miss Lizette. I only hope you mayn't find out their abuses.

Lizette and the Dauphin play; Joseph and the page retire to back and look on.

ST. LEON (*to page and Joseph aside*). Now then, when the Dauphin plays a good move, applaud; when he plays a bad one, applaud doubly; then he won't find it out, and will be pleased with himself and you.

Enter the DUC DE ST. PREUX.

ST. P. I was searching for you, St. Leon; but this is the last place I expected to find you in.

ST. L. Are you not aware that I have been promoted to the sinecure of General Instructor of H.R.H. the Dauphin.

ST. P. That is why I made sure I should not find you in his vicinity.

ST. L. You underrate my zeal and abilities; (*to the Dauphin*) will Your Royal Highness deign to inform Monsieur le Duc de St. Preux why it was I, above all the Court was selected, for the office of General Instructor.

DAU. Because you were certain not to be able to teach me anything.

ST. L. And do I fulfil my duties to Your Royal Highness satisfaction.

DAU. Admirably ; but I have learnt something in spite of you.

ST. P. Your Royal Highness is a Phœnix. You have really learned something, tell us what it is?

DAU. That when a king wears the colours of his people, he ceases to be king.

Jos. Nay, Your Dauphinship, read the lesson backward. The year that a king adopts his people's cause is the first of his reign.

ST. P. Joseph, you talk of what you don't understand. The masses here are nettles, and if not crushed, will inflame the realm.

Jos. In our country, my Lord, if nettles overrun a soil, we blame the ~~former owner~~.

ST. P. St. Leon, matters are really growing serious. You know that we, of the Queen's faction, have done all in our power to ignore the existence of the third estate. We have locked them out of all their places of rendezvous. We suggested to their delegates that they might have to approach the King only on their knees, according to old precedents. " What? if the king commands it," said I.

St. L. And what answered the proud provincials.

St. P. The President Bailly answered, " What ? if twenty-five million of men forbid it ? "

Jos. Bravo, Bailly !

St. L. What insolence.

Jos. Yes, and its greatest insolence is its truth.

St. P. Of course we shall put down these upstarts ; but it will take some days yet, owing to the King's absurd objection to fire on the people.

Dau. The people—what's that ?

Jos. Twenty-five millions of human beings, your Royal Highness, multiplied to double their strength by despair.

Dau. That move checks the king.

St. P. The Archbishop of Paris was compelled to seek Sanctuary yesterday.

Dau. Bishop to Castle's Square.

St. P. The malcontents have spread a rumour that the soldiery are disaffected.

Dau. Now I have lost my knight.

St. P. The Queen gives a Royal fête to-night. She is determined not to encourage the small faction opposed to us, by taking their discontent seriously.

Jos. Twenty-five millions a small faction ! Oh Lor' !

St. P. We are determined not to yield one jot of our position—we will not tax the nobles—we will *not* resign our manorial rights.

Dau. What are our rights ?

Jos. The people wrongs !

Liz. Their wrongs are all they've got, your Royal Highness, so don't grudge them to them.

Dau. Now I've lost my queen, I won't play any more. (*Comes down. They make way for him, and bow as he moves out.*)

Dau. Gentlemen, is there going to be a storm ? I heard an odd noise in the court-yard.

St. L. (*looking out*) It's only some women, your Royal Highness, crying out that they are hungry.

Dau. Hunger ?—What's that ?

Jos. It's what's making the twenty-five million " insolent."

Dau. Poor things ; then I suppose it hurts them. I'll go and fling them out all my toys and sweetmeats. *Exit.*

St. P. The ball has begun—I hear the music of the minuet (*music of Gavotte Heard*), come St. Leon. Let the emissaries of the mob find us dancing to the tune of their menaces.

Jos. (*stops him*) My Lord Duke, for the sake of " Auld Langsyne," those happy days of perquisites and peculation unlimited, permit me to give you a warning ; the danger is greater and nearer than you think.

St. P. The nearer the danger, the lighter my heart—Don't concern yourself for me, Joseph, I shall dance, but it will be with one hand on this. (*touching his rapier.*)

Jos. At least, order a guard to be set around your house, remember it is only a little way off the palace.

St. P. True, my wife and son. I will go at once and ask for one or two of the Royal Bodyguard—for their protection. *Exit.*

Jos. And you, sir, if you have anything you hold precious—next your life—seek some protection for it.

St. L. True, my cellar. I will at once go and ask for a *great* number of the Royal Bodyguard—for my liquor's sake. *Exit.*

Jos. Hip, hip hurrah ! Vive liberty, equality and all the rest of it. Lizette, congratulate me, I am a made man—I may say a ready-made man !

Liz. I don't see any difference in you, Mr. Joseph.

Jos. Not see any difference. Why, look at my new hat ? You may say, " What's in a hat," as Shakespeare says.

Liz. " Your head !—a trifle light as air," as Shakespeare says. You see, Mr. Joseph, I have profited by your instruction !

Jos. Just enough to turn it against me ; how like a woman ! But never mind, Miss Lizette, I am in such good spirits, I could forgive you anything, even for marrying me.

Liz. I could do better. I could forgive you for marrying anyone else.

Jos. Why will a woman always have the last word ?

Liz Out of revenge on Adam, who had the first.

Jos. Talking of Adam, do you know what I am now. I am a *Sans Culotte*.

Liz. A what ?

Jos. A S-a-n-s C-u——

Liz. Hush-h. I don't think you can have looked out that word in the dictionary, Mr. Joseph.

Jos. I've only got my Manuel de Voyage, which tells you how to ask for everything you don't want, in three languages (*looks over a book*); how to ask for a barber, a bookseller, a tailor——

Liz. Of course, *they've* nothing to do with it. I'll show you where to find it in the dictionary with my eyes shut tight ; and since when have you adopted this style of new garment ?

Jos. It's the reward of patriotism, Lizette.

Liz. Make the most of it, for, scanty as it is, it's all the reward you're likely to get.

Jos. You're mistaken. All men are to share, and share alike, and I'm to have a sinecure ; Liberty, Fraternity, Equality—that's our motto.

Liz. Well, Joseph, your motto shall be my motto.

Jos. A motto is a thing that goes round a seal. Let's seal the compact, Lizette.

Enter Piere La Rouge.

Piere. Humph !—Is this a time for trifling, citizen ?

Jos. I was only just—only teaching this young woman the principles of civil freedom.

Piere. Yes, I see.—Here's a letter.

Jos. For whom ?

Piere. Marcelle—Ain't she here, disguised as an aristocrat—A very good disguise too. Danton gave her the jewels and nature a heart as hard as that of any noble among them. She will open the palace doors to us.

Jos. But there'll be no blood shed—will there ?

Piere. Nothing worth mentioning ; but be sure of this —if you show yourself, that worst of enemies, a false friend, *your's* shall be the first blood shed, and if you draw back *now*, it shall be with a knife inside you.   *Exits.*

Liz. Hey day, Mr. Joseph, is this another phase of civil freedom ?

Enter St. Leon *hurriedly.*

St. L. Lizette, come to my assistance, or I am lost. I was bidden to tread a measure with majesty itself, and just when the Blue eye of Austria beamed on me, it beamed also on a black on my nose—the patch that should have been on my chin had got rubbed the wrong way. Pull it right, Lizette, and accept this proof of my gratitude. (*gives her a gold piece and a salute. Joseph twitches her.*)

Liz. Nay, Mr. Joseph, this is only fraternity, you know.

St. L. I will reward you even yet more munificently, Lizette. Come this way, and I will give you—what do think? Why, a place from whence you can see me dancing.

Jos. (*aside*) Lizette, I forbid you to go. Attentions to you, from one of his rank are insults.

Liz. But we are all equal now—this is equality.

Jos. You shan't go, I tell you !

Liz. But I will !—and this is Liberty ! *Exit, laughing.*

Jos. Fraternity, equality, and liberty are all very well in their way, but if this is the way they're going to be applied, blow me if I don't turn a d——d aristocrat (*calls after her.*) Lizette, darling hussy come back, or I'll never see you again, never ! She won't—then I'll—I'll follow her at once, and see what she's up to ! (*stuffs his red cap into his pocket and steals out, wearing St. Leon's dress hat.*)

Enter Marcelle *and* St. Preux.

St. P. I have brought you here, my fair unknown, because it is the study and therefore the least frequented room in the house. (*they sit down.*)

Mar. So you tell me you have never loved.

St. P. Never—until now !

Mar. You can say that ?

St. P. I can swear it !

Mar. And without blushing ! ! ! You must have sworn it very often to have attained such fluency.

Sт. P. Nay, madam, true passion is always fluent.

Mar. Yes, when it is at it's zenith, but as our aquaintance only commenced—let me see—how long ago ?

Sт. P. About half an hour since—which seemed, alas, but so many minutes !

Mar. But granted that you being, as you say, *so* unsophisticated and inexperienced in the tender passion, are able to feel more in half an hour, than an adept could in half his life. Still, we cannot be supposed to be *very* far gone in the ever-new, ever-old story, ca' Love.

Sт. P. There are *some* versions of that story of which a single glimpse is sufficient to make one long to read to the end. (I flatter myself that's prettily said.)

Mar. Well, but when it is finished, I fear you might begin another version! Some readers are insatiable of novelty. No, no, Monsieur, it is evident that you are a proficient in what *you* call " Love ;" but the wisest man that ever lived can learn something from the silliest woman that ever talked, in that particular accomplishment. For one thing, you are *too wise*. Remember that Brutus won an Empire by looking what every true lover looks in the early stage of his complaint ;

Sт. P. And that is——

Mar. A Fool !

Sт. P. I'm beginning to feel like one, if that is anything towards it. Well, Madam, what other symptoms should true Love show !

Mar. True Love stutters when he is most true. You are most eloquennt when most mendacious. True Love stumbles, doesn't know what to do with his hands and feet, looks awkward and feels—divine. You move with ease, look like an aristocrat and feels—like a clown. True Love thinks all the world is turned into one woman, and for that reason all womankind are sacred to him. *You* love all womenkind, and, therefore, no one of them is sacred to you.

Sт. P. But, my dear Madam, don't you think that this true love of yours is a mnch overrated quality ? What is the good of it ? People who feel it (or who fancy they do) are generally very uncomfortable, very cross, very rude, very ill-bred. *Nothing* satisfies them. They're like the English on their travels—paying through the nose for the most trifling accommodation, and always grumbling at it !

MAR. Yes, but when you compare a lady to a story that is to be read, she likes to think that *her* story is to be the " story without an end." Now, there is *no* end for true love, for the story he begins here, he continues in Heaven. But let us leave this subject until it is capable of being discussed with more animation. Give me some proof of your sincerity, such as confession. Tell me somewhat of your past.

ST. P. (*aside*) When a father questions his son of the past, he is thinking of his debts ; when a woman does so, she is inquisitive about his love affairs. Well, Madam, I assure you, I always *mean* to be constant when I begin.

MAR. I fear yours are means to an end—and to a speedy end. What about that story of you and the Marquise de Valcourt ?

ST. P. The Marquise—who—which—oh, I remember —to be sure, yes—a charming woman, she was all soul, and insisted on my hearing three masses a day—I shot her husband—I'm sure that was a perfect proof of devotion—for I got a pistol wound, and made her the fashion.

MAR. What of Lucille St. Foix ?

ST. P. Oh ! Lucille was charming, too—quite irresistable, but ended in being unbearable—it's a way they have !

MAR. What of Claire ?

ST. P. Claire had an equinoctical nature — no one could expect a man to live with a hurricane ; and then she had a trick of stabbing her rivals, which tended to diminish my popularity with your adorable sex.—One lucky—I mean luckless—day, she stormed herself into the river, and I gave her a monument in proportion to the greatness of my relief—I mean grief.

MAR. And what of Marcelle ?

ST. P. Eh ?—what name did you say ?

MAR. Marcelle !—Is the name so uncommon ?

ST. P No, but the feeling is uncommon, with which in my mind, that name is associated—why I nearly loved her once.

MAR. (*scornfully*) Marcelle is grateful for the admission—I mean she, no doubt, would be charmed to know that in return for her utter devotion, you loved her *nearly*—but it is something that one name, at least, awakens some regret.

ST. P. More than regret—remorse! it is as the name of one long dead, which, suddenly spoken strikes awe into the frivolous hours of the living.

MAR. You loved her then!

ST. P. At any rate I thought I did, and that's a greater compliment than I've paid any woman since.

MAR. And yet you deserted her!

ST. P. Not intentionally, but my father interfered, and the country got very dull, and there were a good many royal fêtes to attend—you know a man *can't* break his engagements. Yes—yes, it was all for the best—it is better as it is!

MAR. *No!*

ST. P. Eh?

MAR. No! A thousand times, no! At least not better for her. What did she do?

ST. P. Got over it, I suppose—as I did;—I have reason to believe she took longer to do so.

MAR. Who can say when a woman survives, or merely suppresses her passion.

ST. P. If she feel it she probably shows it—you know the proverb—love and fire cannot be hidden.

MAR. But the love may turn to fire, and then turn on its cause.

ST. P. One can but act for the best.

MAR. Such is the perfection of a man's selfish philosophy that I believe that after Jason had got over those little affairs with Medea and Creusa, he consoled himself with another and wealthier bride, *and* that self-soothing platitude "It's all for the best." From your point of view, all a woman's suffering is for a man's "best"—you are always ready to weigh the possible inconveniences any woman might oocasion you with some petty advantage you desire from her loss.

ST. P. One often thought Alkestis made a great mistake in coming back again!

MAR. (*rising*). Do you mean to insult me Monsieur by (*recovers herself*)—by treading on my gown.

Enter ST. LEON, THORNHILL, DE LA ROCHE-JAQUELEIN, *the* MARQUISE DE ROSELIT, MADAME DE COMEZ, LA COMTESSE DE VIELLERROCHE, &C.

ST. LEO. Ha! ha; Is it not absurd, St. Preux? I have just been giving these ladies a shock—it is said there is an uninvited guest here. A woman of low degree has effected an entrance to the palace, and is going the festivities.

MADAME DE COMEZ. Is it not dreadful to think that I nearly touched the creature?

MADAME DE VIELLEROCHE. And that I saluted her, in the dance. Pah!

MADAME DE ROSELIT. And I spoke to her—taking her for the Comte d'Artois favourite, and she is only a common peasant woman after all.

DE LA ROCHE. Is there anything against her?

ST. L. Nothing that I know of morally.

DE LA ROCHE. It seems she is an uncommon woman.

Enter JOSEPH.

Jos. I have a letter to deliver from a member of the National Assembly, formerly called the Third Estate; my directions are to give it into the hands of Marcelle.

ST. PREUX. Where is ⎫
DE LA ROCHE. Who is ⎬ Marcelle?
ST. LEON. What is ⎭

MAR. I will tell you—she is the firebrand of disaffection —she is the life and soul of the communistic party— she is the ideal of a politician; pitiless and unscrupulous; she is the mouth-piece of starvation and despair, is a woman of the people who has been wronged by your order, and who will presently be avenged by her own.

Mme. DE ROSE. Pray have her found and turned out of the place; I feel as frightened as though a black beetle were crawling about the path.

MAR. (*unmasking*) You have not far to seek—I am she.

ALL. Marcelle!

MAR. (*to St. Preux*) And you did not recognise me?

ST. P. No; but I was certain it was some one who loved me—you were so very bitter.

Mar. Francois, when we last met, my heart was soft with the memory of the past. *Now*, I have a past to look back on, which is so black, that its shadow is thrown over the future of all connected with me. Faith, honour, hope—you murdered them all. And now even love is dead, and I only live by the flame and nourishment of my hate.

St. P. It's a matter of no consequence one way or the other, but you must excuse my not believing you. When a woman speaks that word love, it is because she yet feels it.

Mar. I have told you that I hate you.

St. P. Love or hate, it's all the same with a woman!

Mar. I hate, and I warn you.

St. P. Against whom?

Mar. Against myself. Oh, you smile. Wait, wait— that smile may cost you dear. I will set against it the years of bitter tears, of sickly hope, of black despair. I will weigh them in the balance when *I* am the arbiter of your fate. Your smile against my agony. If, of all your evil life you repent nought else, be sure of this, you *shall* repent.

St. P. You talk wildly——

Mar. I feel wildly, and you, poor painted fools of the Court, listen to my voice, for it is one of myriads. This man trifled with me, and it is dangerous to trifle with a woman; but to trifle with a people is fatal. It is the monkey playing with the tiger. It is the children of a nation that learns its lessons; and the men of to-day were children when they starved under your infamous taxes. When the whole air of our beautiful France reeked with our miseries and your sins—you have starved our bodies and destroyed our souls. We believe only in vileness and corruption—thanks to your example. We have lost our own sense of virtue in contemplating your infamy. Ah, gentlemen, when you were grinding us under foot, why did you not guess that you were undermining your own foothold?

St. Leon. Really, madame, you seem terribly in earnest —now I haven't been in earnest for years!

Mar. Then, Monsieur, you have lived too long.

St. Leo. Really she is quite uncivil. I don't envy St. Preux his conquest—some sportsmen have a fancy for savage prey—tigresses, and the like. I prefer the tame domestic bird which you can delude by feeding it one day, while you prepare to shoot it on the next.

Dr. Thor. Do not mind her, gentlemen. She is ill—Mad. She does not mean what she says. Marcelle, come away. A few hours of rest and peace will restore you.

Mar. Rest—peace. No—I leave those words in the past, in the old sunny paths of Brittany (*suddenly to St. Preux*). Francois, do you remember that path? (*he shakes his head*).

Mar. (*impatiently*) Oh, you *cannot* forget it; the fallen tree in the corner—the primroses that grew in tufts between the branches—you have some beautiful flowers here, but I like primroses best; so did *you* then, Francois; you said you thought the angels wore them in their hair.

St. P. Yes, but I don't believe in angels now.—St. Leon it is time for us to attend Her Majesty, she holds a Court, ere the festivities end, to allow her royal subjects to make their adieux.

St. Leo. Wouldn't miss it for the universe.

Dr. Thor. It is well that you are so devoted to your Queen, she may require it, if what Marcelle says be correct, you may even be called on to die for her.

St. Leo. I will do better; I will live for her. As for devotion, we Frenchmen have sufficient confidence in ourselves to leave all the devotion to the other sex—they can provide enough for both. It is but the poor Queen who *couldn't* do without me.

Dr. Thor. Indeed, what is your vocation.

St. Leo. To educate the unformed and uninformed debutantes to bow and curtsey properly. Good heavens, sir, do you think that any monarchy could exist if its heads were outraged by such extraordinary genuflexions as the bourgeoisie practice. I have been to England. I have seen your village children make their obeisances—it was as if a flock of ducks waddled past, and then suddenly dived! Such a sight would have killed a French-woman.

DR. THORN. (*drily*). Don't trouble yourself. You must earn the gratitude of the poor before they can acknowledge it.

ST. LEO. It is the privilege of us aristocrats to earn nothing. Come, ladies.

Each takes a hand of the ladies, and turn up the stage. Marcelle, who has been watching from the centre, comes down.

MAR. It is the signal—hark! The Queen will hold no court to-day.

ALL. How!

MAR. Do you not hear that noise? Ha! you have only known the sound of the footsteps of the poor, when they trudged for you in the loneliness of labour and want. You did not guess how terrible the wooden shoes could be when they crowded together—how ominous the thunder of their march when they seek the tyrants who will now be their victims. Monsieur, (*to Thornhill*) you have shewn me much kindness. Take my advice by way of re-payment—go back home at once.

DR. THOR. To Paris.

MAR. No, no. As soon throw yourself into the lake of fire. Go back to your own country where law and order yet guard English homes and English lives. Where you respect the living and reverence the dead. I too have visited England like Monsieur here, but I noticed something more than the awkwardness of a few rustics. I noticed the grace of the union, of their great power. Heaven, love and law. Go back to your churches where men's faces still dare to look upwards! to your law, self-imposed, and therefore ungrudgingly obeyed. You have a minister who has made boyhood famous, and the name of William Pitt old in the future. You have a monarch whose sympathy is as large as the people's sorrow, and whose hand is ever stretched out, not to smite, but to console. Go, leave us to carnage and anarchy, the mob are as wild brutes escaped, in the darkness of night, from bars of oppression and rods of fire; and, in the tumult, they see neither the face of heaven, nor that of friends.

St. P. She is right, the courtyard is bristling with pikes. I must go to my wife.

La Roche. And I to my Sovereign.

Mar. (Stop them.) Too late, too late, Monsieur; the Queen is safe for the present—her guards have died to enable her to escape to the king's apartments. Listen! At last the people's voices have reached royalty, and they reach it in the form of a death knell. Francois, your house is destroyed. Your wife and child are being taken prisoners to Paris.

St. P. I will follow. I will release them; friend, do you rejoice in my torture.

Mar. Ha, ha, ha. I see you really *can* feel—perhaps *at last* you understand what I felt when we parted; your misery is as great, your helplessness as complete *now* as mine were *then*; I promised you that I would return Francois, and that on *this* day I would remember *that*. Do you see those flames yonder—they seem to burn fierce joy into my heart, for they represent all that is left of your house. I am avenged, and at last I can sing once more.

(*Puts on a red cap, seizes a tricolour flag, both passed to her through the window, and sings the "Marseillaise."*)

CURTAIN.

ACT III.

SCENE 1.—*A corridor in* Marcelle's *House.* Joseph *discovered sorting her letters.*
Marcelle's *door* L.   *Entrance* R.

Jos. Here's a lot of them—invitations to cut off people's heads seem to come as thickly to Marcelle, as assignations used to my master—a short life and a merry one seems the motto in France just now—the worst of it is, one's own head feels quite shaky from sympathy.

Enter Pierre Larosse, he places his hand on Joseph who stares.

PIER. Citizen—I've got a job for you ; the committee of public safety are anxious to test your sincerity—they therefore demand as a proof of it, that you officiate as executioner to one of the worst of your former tyrants.

Jos. Not Lizette !

PIER. No, not Lizette *yet :* The order refers to the aristocrat known as the Vicomte St. Leon, he is to be your first experiment—if you succeed well you may be rewarded by a permanent appointment—if you flinch, or show any signs of distaste to your duty, you will have to take his place—in that case *I* shall have the pleasure of officiating.

Jos. Don't mention it ; wouldn't give you the trouble for the world—not that I have ever decapitated anything before, excepting corks.

PIER. You'll find this nearly as light work—your subject is coming this way now.

Jos. *(looking off)* So he is, does he know what is going to happen to him ?

PIER. Hasn't an idea of it—he fancies he has made an impression on Marcelle, and that he is therefore safe— he is coming now to seek her.

Jos. Poor fellow, I mean—villainous aristocrat—I think I'll go, I'd rather not face him—I'm no hypocrite, and I don't care to take off my hat to a gentleman whose head I have to perform a similar operation on.

PIER. *(stopping him)* On the contrary, you had best see him and break it to him gently.

Jos. How can one break such a thing gently.

PIER. Well, he must know it sooner or later, and it would be an act of kindness to prepare him—remember it's your task or mine—I should make nothing of such a trifle, good-day citizen—I promise you *I* won't flinch if they give *me* the job—perhaps, in case of accidents, I'd better say " au revoir" *(exit.)*

Jos. Axe-i-dents—indeed—oh dear ! Now I've always prided myself on my manners, and my lofty method of announcing an earl, has often made him ashamed that he wasn't a Duke—but this sort of announcement I've no experience in, and it's difficult to tell a man you mean to take his head without seeming to be taking a liberty. How am I to combine the sternness of the Patriot with the urbanity of the British Butler? I must quench the Butler with the Brutus when I'm declaiming against these aristocrats at a safe distance from them. I feel like a tradesman disposing of soiled stock at a sacrifice, and could knock off any amount of them—when I'm alongside of them, the Butler gets uppermost, and I can't help resuming my traditional servility. But I must harden myself to my task. Citizen *(roughly to* ST. Leon, *who enters jauntily).*

ST. LEO. Oh, is that you, friend Joseph!

JOS. Friend—really he speaks very nicely, and just as I had insulted him, by callling him "Citizen," too! But I mustn't be civil—I must remember that I'm a Patriot—yes, Citizen!?

ST. LEO. Could you get me such a thing as a glass of wine?

JOS. Wine, sir? yes-sir. *(aside* After all I can afford to pour out a glass of wine for a gentleman whom I shall soon leave with nothing to pour it down in!)

ST. LEO. I understand that Marcelle has taken you and Lizette under her care. Now my object in calling here is to ask her to do as much for me. You know I had the discernment to appreciate her charms at a very early stage of our acquaintance; I offered to be her Bacchus; *(helping himself to the wine.)*

JOS. I've always heard that Bacchus supplied his own wine!

ST. LEO. My friend, he did not live in the times of Liberty, Fraternity and Equality—Liberty, Fraternity and Equality have got at my cellar, and have left nothing but empty bottles. Have you heard what they mean to do with my poor friend, St. Preux?

JOS. St. Preux? Yes-sir; they'll cut off his head to-morrow, sir!

ST. LEO. Will they, really; (excellent wine this).—Well, well, he was a good sort of man.

JOS. We met with worse aristocrats.

ST. LEO. But full of faults!

Jos. It's hardly worth while reckoning up, if he's going to end them all tomorrow.

St. Leo No, only it's a comfort to think of his faults. Under the circumstances it might have been worse—they might have selected a worthier victim, and found more difficulty in absolving themselves for the crime !

Jos. Yes, they might have took my head or yours— (*aside*) they gave me the choice, and of two evils I chose the least.

St. Leo. You don't mean to say they have thought of injuring you. Why, you are of their own party !

Jos. Yes, sir ; and there's nothing like one's own wife, or one's own party, for finding out one's weakest points, and aggravating them accordingly. My party found out that I had no taste for pulling down houses or cutting off heads.

St. Leo. Then why become a republican ?

Jos. I was a republican in England, sir ; but that's very different—you see I knew that the king and the laws were quite safe there, so I didn't care how much I talked against 'em ; in fact my notion of being a republican was to keep a Public on funds provided by appreciative Co-patriots, or by timid ministerial agents ; but I never wished to " wade through slaughter " to my Public ! The sight of blood makes me feel sick. My party found that out, and it sealed my doom.

St. Leo. What, my poor fellow, your doom is sealed and you've got to suffer too !

Jos. Well, I sha'n't like the job.

St. Leo. No, of course not—and yet, Joseph, there are consolations to be found even in your situation !

Jos. Yes. I might be in somebody else's situation ; but I'm glad you can take it in this way. It will make it easier to me.

St. Leo. I flatter myself I can exhibit philosophic fortitude whenever a friend needs it, Joseph ; and in spite of your originally humble station in life, I look on your present position as one that exalts you.

Jos. Of course it's an honour one way, but I fear it may be awkward—you see I've no experience.

St. Leo. No, of course not—a man can die but once.

Jos. No; but he may be a long time doing it, and that would be painful to all parties.

St. Leo. Then I can only exhort you to remember the examples of stoicism set you by the martyrs of all generations. Think of the benefit it may prove to your country ! your being in such a terrible position will bring home to your fellow radicals the horrors of this political immorality !

Jos. Well, sir, to do 'em justice there isn't one of 'em would fancy the job—but what's the good of my making a fuss about it.

St. Leo. None, the slightest I should say; and as you may not have an opportunity of doing me any service again.

Jos. No, sir, I shall never do for you again after to-morrow.

St. Leo. I wish you'd tie the bow of my cravatte for me—I'm about to see Marcelle, and I must look my best.

Jos. Yes-sir—you've a nice small throat, sir.

St. Leo. So the ladies say—it's contour always makes a great impression.

Jos. Ah, it's my turn to make an impression now !

St. Leo. Well Joseph, I commisserate you, and if it will console you to have my forgiveness for any little wrong done me in the matter of corked wine or cold ragôuts, let it console you to know that I forgive you fully and freely.

Jos. You're sure of that.

St. Leo. Yes, on my honour.

Jos. You'll forgive me everything ?

St. Leo. Everything.

Jos. This will give me strength to perform my duty.

St. Leo. I'm glad of that; whatever is worth doing at all is worth doing well.

Jos. I will do it as well as I can ; but I am very sorry for you—especially now you're so affable—I never thought to live to hear Joseph Merryweather called "friend" by a Vicomte—it makes me more unwilling to exterminate the solitary specimen that has done it.

St. Leo. You exterminate ? why isn't it you who are going to be killed ?

Jos.   No, it's I who am going to kill.

St. Leo.   Kill what—who ?

Jos.   Why you, to be sure ! didn't you understand that ? how dull of you !

St. Leo.   I was in hope—I mean I thought that it was· you who were to suffer—it's impossible it can be true— sacrifice me ! a' St. Leon—my head would be an irreparable loss to France.

Jos.   Such heads as yours have been a loss to France long enough, and now she is determined to get some amusement out of 'em, at least my Lord Vicomte that's the patriotic view of it.

St. Leo.   It can't—it sha'n't be true.

Jos.   Calm yourself, remember there are consolations to be found, even by one in your position.

St. Leo.   Yes, by my friends—no, doubt not by me— I can never, never be consoled for the loss of myself, never ! I never loved any one half so much ! or so long.

Jos.   But recall the examples of stoicism.

St. Leo.   Examples of fiddlesticks.

Jos.   You recalled them easily enough just now.

St.   Leo.   But that was for you—as for you vile murderer who seek to imbrue your hands in innocent blood.

Jos.   Innocent fiddlesticks.

St. Leo.   Let me see Marcelle—let me at once clench the effect I produced on that estimable woman.

Jos.   She is enjoying herself down at the conciergerie, looking over the last convoy of prisoners brought in for execution !

St. Leo.   Horrible wretch—I mean divine heroine— but she will see me when she returns ?

Jos.   Well, she has so many applications—if she entertained them all, she would have to provide half France with sticking plaster for the neck.

St. Leo.   At least if—if—that awful event should occur, and you are the hideous—I mean innocent instrument, promise me you'll delay the proceedings as long as possible—the ladies are sure to get up a petition for me !

Jos.   If you were a desperate criminal whose talent lay in wife murder, I've no doubt but that they would ; but I'm afraid you ain't wicked enough to be spared.

St. Leo.   Oh, but I'll be wickeder.

Jos.   Yes, what is worth doing at all, is worth doing well, as you said—I'll remember your advice when I come to draw the fatal bolt.

(St. Leon *moves hastily towards entrance door*, Joseph *stops him.*)

Jos.   *You* needn't bolt—I'm not going to begin yet—your cravat has come untied, let me fasten it tighter for you.

St. Leo.   *(shrinking)* Ugh—no I thank, I prefer it loose, mine is a very sensitive skin—keep your hands off, I won't wait for Marcelle now, I'll call again. *(going)*

Jos.   *(following him)* You know you said you forgave me.

St. Leo.   I'm d——d if I will.   *(exit.)*

Jos.   How ungrateful some people are—I'm sure I put it as civilly as I could—If he objects so much in anticipation, what will he do in fact; really it's horrid work—I've half a mind—I've a whole mind to throw up the job—I will too—I'll get passports from Marcelle for me and Lizette, and we'll run away to England to-night.   If there are not many Patriots there, there are a vast of Publics which is nearly the same, only pleasanter !   There, secure in the serene enjoyment of a popular monarchy, just laws, and ancient constitution we'll luxuriate in theoretical democracy at a safe distance from its practical and very unpleasant effects—*me* carve off a human head ! never—but if the fates and Lizette are propitious, I'll carve my christmas beef for Mrs. Merryweather this winter in England, and, as the years go on, if the fates and Lizette are propitious, I'll carve christmas beef for an indefinite number of little Merryweathers'—the theoretical democrats of the future.   *exit* (L.)

Act III.   Scene II.—*A cell in the Conciergerie—Time, evening—gradually changing to moonlight—window to* R.H. *door* C.   *small stone jug, a piece of black bread, chair, a pallet* L. H., *and on it* St. Preux, *discovered heavily chained and asleep.*

St. P.   *(awaking, calls)* Jacques, Charles !   what lazy rascals those valets of mine are not to bring the hot water ; (*seeing jug*) halloa—umph ! it seems what water there is, is cold and very little of it—decidedly the Republic doesn't wash—Hi, gaoler, what's that for? (*pointing to jug.*)

Enter Pierre Larosse, C.

PIER. (*gruffly*) To drink, fool.

St. P. It smells very harmless—a little *too* harmless ; my good friend, I've tried every novelty in the world excepting that of drinking water in its native impurity, and I'm afraid it would give me a cold inside—couldn't you ? eh ? (PIERRE *shakes his head;* ST. PREUX *drops a gold piece in the jug*) you'd give even a canary bird a rusty nail to prevent its having the pip—pray let it taste better when you come back—and what's this ? (*holding up the bread.*)

PIER. Your breakfast.

St. P. Why, I wouldn't insult my dog by offering it to him, and he wouldn't eat it if I did !

PIER. I dare say not, but *we've* had no better breakfast for years past. The grand nobles took care of their dogs, and never noticed that starvation was making *us* feel like wolves.

St. P. It's nothing to me what you feel.

PIER. No, and *that's* why you're here—ho, ho.

St. P. But I be——

PIER. Hush, you know what you be now, but you don't know what you may *not* be to-morrow.

St. P. (*flinging aside the crust*) Well then, I'll leave that as a legacy to the Republic wolves, having sharp teeth may be able to bite it.

PIER. Ah, you should have worked for it, then it would have tasted sweet.

St. P. Have you got such a thing as a barber in this um—establishment, my chin feels so uncomfortable.

PIER. Don't trouble about that, it won't be for long.

St. P. I beg your pardon, my beard grows uncommonly long if it isn't shaved—doesn't the Republic *ever* shave ?

PIER. No, but it's very fond of hairdressers, one they chiefly employ will cut your hair soon !

St. P.   The devil he will.

Pier.   No, the headsman—he will—he makes *one job*
of it, you know ! *he* is the leader of fashion now—he has
put *down* perukes and long hair, and only patronises
crops—he likes to see the shape of the throat.

St. P.   That's a very handsome bunch of keys, might
I ask what object they serve ?

Pier.   To lock up the enemies of the Republic ; those
villains who seek to evade fraternal legislation and to en-
slave the Republic, which is a free institution.

St. P.   So it seems—makes a little *too* free sometimes,
I think—one comfort is, it seems to have a large number
of enemies—I hope *all* of them are not going to experience the last extremity of fraternal equity—are many of
us condemned ?

Pier.   Dozens.

St. P.   Is there no chance for me—for such.

Pier.   Well, I should be very sorry to hold shares in
their insurance companies ; ha, ha.

St. P.   Any—any one of—my name ?

Pier.   Well, I've got a memorandum some where in
my pocket (*pulls out a very long roll*).

St. P.   One would think that you had got my tailor
as well as my hairdresser waiting for me to settle my account—but the question is, am I in that list or not ?

Pier.   Oh, you're sure to be *there*—the question is, do
you come among the S's or the P's ?

St. P.   The Republic won't wash—probably the Republic can't spell, try the P's.

Pier.   There you are, isn't the name beautifully written—
I did that—I was educated on your estate by the Curé,
and this is the first good use I've been able to put it to.

St. P.   Ah, h, h—yes—a signal proof of my folly in
fostering a nettle to sting my foot.

Pier.   You'll be in what you call "good society"—all
the noblest names in France are bere—it's as long as a
list of guests at a Royal Court, only it's a court, ho, ho,
of death !

St. P.   My man, I'll give you the weight of these
chains in gold if you will contrive to blot my name out
of that list for the space of another week.

Pier. So you're afraid (St. P. *raises his hand*) ah, keep back will you, or I'll call the guard.

St. P. Call the guard to one man—well do, *I* am *not* afraid to die ; but I do fear to die before I have learnt some intelligence about those whom my death will leave widowed and orphaned.

Pier. Your bribe is of no avail; I have not power to help you—but still, if you like to hand me such few valuables as may be left about you, I'll give you a more valuable hint.

St. P. Take them. (*pulls out money, chain, snuffbox, ring, &c.*) There is my wife's portrait in that box—my boy's hair in that locket—but you'll allow me to take out their contents ?

Pier. Of course—*they're* not worth anything—but that cross !

St. P. That cross, I concealed before I was taken prisoner by the fraternity ; it is the cross of St. Louis, the highest order a French monarch can confer on a noble of his realm, and rather than see it defiled by the unclean touch of his majesty's unclean enemies, I would trample it to fragments *thus*, thinking it less dishonoured by a gentleman's heel than a sans-culottes hand.

Pier. The sans-culottes hands are too busy about gentlemen's necks just now to care about other trinkets— but here is my hint ; you know Marcelle—get speech of her—*she* is the queen of our revels, she is the adored of Danton ; she can if she will play with heads just as *you* may have once played with hearts—*she* can save you if she likes, only I don't know why she should like, and it's hardly worth while to trouble her about such a trifle— however, I'll let her know, but don't buoy yourself up by hope, she's very busy just now—it's *our* season for enjoyment you know—ho, ho !

St. P. Well, you seem to make the most of it.

Pier. Yes, I like seeing you here—such as you have kept France in gaol long enough ; *now* the trappers are trapped. I hope you'll have a good night, you may not have many more of them, so *you* had better make the most of it.

St. P. *(aside)* It *cannot* be so near as he says—I feel so well, so strong *(goes to window)* I can only see house-tops and a few inches of sky, but I think I never appreciated a view so much in my life ! There goes a bird—going home to roost I dare say, to think that I should have come to envy a sparrow ! a month ago I should have shot it *(how this arm hurts)*. I don't think I'll ever shoot or cage anything again *(if I get the chance)*. I begin to feel rather faint and sick, I wonder why ? perhaps I'm hungry ! I did not think novelty could be so disagreeable, I wonder what became of that crust *(looks about)* I really don't believe I could touch it, but—good Heavens, I hope he hasn't taken it away ! no, here it is *(eats ravenously)*. It isn't so very bad after all, nevertheless, if I ever get free again, all the poor on my estate shall have white bread, and as much as they like of it—so I am to appeal to Marcelle, appeal to a tigress to forego the taste of blood—appeal to a woman whom you have forgotten to love ! well, it is her turn now, and she may forget to save one. Ah me, if one could but treat the past as one does a pledged trinket, and take it out of pawn to futurity some of us might be redeemed yet.

He sits L. H. *head bent and hands clasped,* MARCELLE *appears, door,* C. MARCELLE *enters (behind him) from* C.

MAR. Pale, chained and sad, that is well—he will think of me now ; he forgot my love, he will not forget my revenge. I have worked for this, I have rejoiced ; I do rejoice, and yet—the blows I have dealt seem to rebound on me and strike me to the heart. *(coldly)* I am here citizen, you wished to see me ?

St. P. Ah, it is you, I thought—I hoped you would come.

MAR. On what did you base your hope ?

St. P. You have kept tryst with me ere now, Marcelle.

MAR. And you have forgotten to do so ere now—perhaps you'll remember this assignation better than those of yore ; chains and prison walls appeal more forcibly to the memory than primroses and wood walks. I lost my heart then, you will lose your head now, and we are quits.

Sᴛ. P.   And is the nightmare, revenge, sweeter than the day-dream of love, Marcelle? are you satiated with my sufferings, do they make you happier?

Mᴀʀ.   *Yes*, a hundred times *yes*; for they make us *one* again.   I have been alone in my agony for ten weary years; now my destroyer shares it, and I am no longer desolate.

Sᴛ. P.   I at least did not design the evil I wrought you—I could not help loving you, but your hate has been systematic, you have robbed me of all—King, country, home, wife and children—all are gone.

Mᴀʀ.   And did *you* not rob me of anything? when you dethroned a soul from hope was *your* deed less than treason—when you fired it to madness was it less than arson—when you left it a black ruin was it less than murder.

Sᴛ. P.   I did all I could to atone—I would have given—

Mᴀʀ.   Hush! do not dare to speak of any compensation unworthy the *all* I gave you; if you can give me back my joy in the sun—the song in my thoughts that kept tune with the spring birds—the conscience that made me feel heaven in my heart, and reverence myself for the feeling—then I will admit that you can give me compensation.

Sᴛ. P.   You women take these things too seriously. How could I have done otherwise? I was responsible to my name, my position, my class, for the woman I selected to participate in them.

Mᴀʀ.   And were you true to your responsibilities as a lover, a friend, a human being, when you cast me aside like a weed on the roadway? did you forget that *he* who creates the weed is the judge of its destroyer?

Sᴛ. P.   Forgive me, Marcelle—for a woman's reason—not because I deserve, but because I so much *need* forgiveness. (*putting out his hand.*)

Mᴀʀ.   I cannot forgive because I cannot forget (*she puts aside his hand, he winces*). Oh, you are wounded, oh, Francois, does it hurt you much?

Sᴛ. P.   It is nothing—and I killed the rascal who in-
flicted it—that's one comfort ; if they had given me a
little more time I would *have* ——

Mᴀʀ.   Repented—oh, Francois say that you repent
of all.

Sᴛ. P.   I would have killed them all and repented
afterwards.

Mᴀʀ.   You have but little time left, in which to destroy others or yourself, your doom is sealed, Francois ;
the life which has worked so much sorrow ! the wealth
which rarely worked good, are alike confiscated ; by to-
morrow night all that remains of you will be a scarcely
remembered name.

Sᴛ. P.   So soon (*sits, covers face with hands.*)

Mᴀʀ.   Yes, it seems strange does it not—*to-day* you
fear, you think, you hope, in fire you *live*—you hear the
clank of your fetters, even *that* sound is sweeter than
none—you can look at me, you who first awoke the divi-
nity of love in my face, and who have branded it with the
cruelty of despair—but cruel as I seem, I do not laugh
with the savage levity of the mob that will press around
you to-morrow to see how an aristocrat meets life's last
in dignity.

Sᴛ. P.   Your allies the mob, are very strong no doubt ;
they can strip the Duke of his possessions—they can
destroy the *man*, but they are as impotent to degrade the
gentleman as they are powerless to imitate him !

Mᴀʀ.   You speak proudly.

Sᴛ. P.   Pride is the one heritage of my patrimony
which your friends *cannot* reach ! you say by to-morrow
night I shall only survive in name—but it will be in *my
own name*, understand ; many sins have blackened the fame
of St. Preux, but never has it been blanched by the dis-
graceful pallor of a white feather !

Mᴀʀ.   Your blood is noble, but is it not also human—
have you no thought of your wife and child ? Ah, when in
the dreams of ʏᴏᴜʀ ʟᴀsᴛ sʟᴇᴇᴘ ᴛʜɪs ɴɪɢʜᴛ, you see
their piteous eyes—when you feel their cheeks wet with
tears against your own—when you hold out your arms
with a giant effort to rescue them from insult and death,
and awake to find this vacant blackness—these heavy

chains—will not your spirit break *then*—will you not gnash your teeth to think that I, Marcelle, your and their bitterest enemy have seen this day the faces *you* will never see again.

St. P.   You have seen them—then they live, they are safe—huzzah, (*flinging himself at* MARCELLE'S *feet*) oh, bless you, Marcelle, for those words—oh, blessed face which has seen *theirs* ! Marcelle, say it again—tell me of them, and I will worship you as never woman was worshipped before.

MAR.   (*dreamily*) There was a man knelt to me once, for what did he pray—a flower that was on my breast—for my heart—my honour—my life—I conceded all, and So I am here, an outcast and a murderess—Francois, in my youth I *could* not say no to you—now I *will* not say yes.

St. P.   Marcelle, for the love of *heaven.*

MAR.   The heaven of which *you* have made me despair.

St. P.   For the sake of the love we bore each other *once.*

MAR.   FOOL to use that word "*once*" to a woman whose love is eternal !

St. P.   Is it eternal ? then love me to the end, and comfort me now ! look Marcelle, I am alone, helpless—no other can give me a tender look, a loving word—you who cherished me when I was happy, rich powerful, you—a woman.*cannot* desert me now in my hour of need, in the shadow of death ; I concede all that you can ask—I own I treated you infamously, I will even own I deserved all my fate—surely it should console any woman to hear that *she* was always right and *he* always wrong—what more can I say ?

MAR.   Less, would have pleaded your cause better. Oh, Francois, cannot you guess that the next sweetest speech to I love you now, is "I loved you then."

St. P.   I gave you my first, and *that* is a man's best love ; I know now how little the gift was worth, but at least it represented *all* the worth that there was in me ; can you not forgive me, Marcelle, for having once loved you too well ?

MAR. Yes, but *never* for having ceased to do so ! death however cancels all debts, and my debt of revenge is nearly void—adieu, Francois. *(music.)*

ST. P. Marcelle, you will tell me of my son—*(she pauses)* you will tell me of her—of my wife ?

MAR. No more ! I do not taunt your agony with a smile as you once did mine—but neither will I brighten it with consolation.

ST. P. For pity sake !

MAR. *No,* you have made my heart as a lurid fire which scatters every tender thought you would fain foster there.

ST. P. At least give her a message from me ?

MAR. I will—I will tell her that your first love and your last thought were *mine*. *(curtain)*

Music to close of curtain.

A corridor in MARCELLE'S *house, a window* R. L. *Entrance to room* L. *Exit from corridor* R. *She is pale and haggard— she carries a rosary, she is all in white with a scarlet ribbon in her hair, rich white silk skirt and a white bournous.*

MAR. I have slept and I have dreamed *(shudders)* a terrible dream, I dreamt that it *was all over,* and that I could no longer say " Forgive me, Francois," to living ears—then the dream changed—he smiled and came towards me, in the wood where we met, but it was dark; there was no sun in that wood, and I tried to call him, but my lips were set fast with all the life of my past love throbbing hotly in my breast I leapt forward to clasp his hands, and lo, they were cold ! cold !! cold !!! I scorned his agony—I mocked his best and purest thoughts—that best which sorrow can sometimes create on the ruins of joy. I fancied I was avenging myself— but in my dream I knew that he was avenged on me— now that he stands face to face with eternal light, how far off all the dark turbulence of love and anger must seem to him—yet if I saved him to what end would it be? He would live blessed in the love of his children *and his wife*, while *(throws aside the cross and beads)* no ! he shall die—aha, it is *she* who murders him, not I, she thrusts herself between me and every gleam of mercy, for I *thought* of mercy. In the cool pause between day and night, when earth seems to be hushed that heaven may listen, then the conscience trembles as though reborn in the pure breast of a child, and my wrong waxes less and my sin greater ; (*softly*) it is *then*, too, I remember how dear he was—it is then I hear the whistle of the thrush in a past summer, and *feel* the sunbeams in which the peasants go to mass up the hill side, striking on his down bent head while he whispers "love me, Marcelle ; love me always!" Hark, what noise is that ? ah, *it is the guillotine ! !* they are erecting it for HIM—for my lover—(*goes to window*) there it is standing out black against God's bright worlds' of stars, and by to-morrow's light it will be beaten against by a raging crowd; the soldiery will guard, the mob will insult their victim— but he will be tranquil I know, quiet as one whose race is proud and whose hope is over ; but if he hear a child's voice laughing in the crowd *that* will make him wince, for he knows not how he leaves his own ! Aha— you will remember me then Francois ! But yet if so, remember to pity me, for my fate is harder than yours— you will die, but I shall survive—survive to recal you like *this*—pale—stern, drawing near the hideous doom *I* have secured to you. "Love me always, Marcelle"— was it he who spoke thus ? kneeling at my feet—*he* who is to kneel *there* under the executioner's hands ! HE SHALL NOT TOUCH HIM—After all he is a gentleman and he was my lover ; if he could but die with his face set brightly against his foe, or with loving arms about him, soothing the bitterness of the death grip, but to perish by foul hands—to be cast out like carrion to the darkness—never—never—the love that destroyed. me shall save him yet (*clock strikes*), there is not much time ; in two hours he must be free, and I occupy his place—he will escape—he will be blithe as a lark winging its way heavenward, and the hand he wounded will have opened his prison and pointed out the beacon of home and safety. (*music*). For *him* there will be warm welcomes, and perchance length of happy days—while for me ?—Ah well, for me there will at least be—forgetfulness. (*gets her cloak, and returns to snatch up her beads and cross.*) Time shortens—I have none left in which to say farewell to my few friends, and but little in which to pray and repent. Perchance the present will absolve the past, and when I mount the scaffold to face death, knowing that he for whom I die is journeying as swiftly as his heart can speed him to another woman. In that supreme moment Heaven may forgive the sin—for the sake of the sacrifice. (*exit*).

ACT III. SCENE III.—*Outside a door of the Conciergerie, a mob is crowded round it. Soldiers protect the entrance. Cries of* "Where is the prisoner?" "Bring out the aristocrat?"

PIERRE LAROSSE *unlocks the door.*

PIER. But where is Marcelle, citizens? Why is she not here to enjoy her triumph? This man was her especial enemy. (*cries of* "Bring him out, bring him out;" "*To* death with him.")

PIER. Ah, well, she's sure to be here directly—hate gives a woman wings.

Opens the door, MARCELLE *appears cloaked, and a hood over her face.*

MAR. And Love fetters a woman with shackles. You asked for Marcelle—I am here, Pierre La Rosse. *Cries of* "But where is the prisoner?" "Where is the accused aristocrat?"

MAR. Escaped, far beyond your reach by this time—safe in the heaven of re-union with his wife and child.

PIER. And by your means—is it Marcelle, who has betrayed herself and her people?

(*Cries and yells of* "Down with Marcelle; to death with the traitoress. *The crowd make a rush at her—the soldiers form a guard round her.*"

PIER. Marcelle, you are lost. What fiend possessed you, that you should have made this sacrifice?

MAR. My friend—I think you misunderstand the impelling influence—it is one's good angel who prompts self-sacrifice.

PIER. The cowardly wretch, to let you take his place.

MAR. Not so—he would have been here now had I not sworn that my life was safe—that you would not, *could* not hurt me !

PIER. But you will die, Marcelle.

MAR. And do you think *that* will hurt me ? The only consolation for my past life, I find in the manner of my death. I loved and I hated that man—that was the earthly part of me—I saved him, and that was divine. Do not trust the sophist's of science, who would fain substitute a cold illiberal light, for the ineffable glow which comes from Heaven. If but one of man's nobler qualities existed, it would defy doubt and baffle scepticism. From the moment I forgave, I regained my hope of forgiveness. My friends, farewell—I go to a bloodless Republic—Forgive me, if you think I wronged you when I redeemed myself by a love strong enough to purify its baser elements ; a love yet greater even than its wrongs, and fearless even unto death

CURTAIN.

FINIS.